'How old are you?' Alain's eyes were like grey flint, but Jassy saw with some small satisfaction the outline of her fingers raising a puffy, angry weal across his cheek.

'Twenty-seven. Not that it's anything to do with you.'

'Oh, I think you will find,' his voice was smooth— he had himself well under control again now, 'that everything to do with Mademoiselle Jacinth Elizabeth Powers is to do with me. Twenty-seven, and yet you have not married. Why is that, I wonder?'

'Does every woman have to? Does it offend your male love of neatness if any one of us is allowed to float around unattached?'

He shrugged. 'A simple question.'

'Well, let's just say I'm choosy, then. Mr Right hasn't happened to cross my path yet.'

'And would you recognise him if he did?'

'Oh, I think so.' And he wouldn't be six feet of infuriatingly arrogant overbearing Frenchman, for a start!

Books you will enjoy
by RACHEL FORD

BELOVED WITCH

Returning to the Manor stirred up some bittersweet memories for Melissa—young love, and her own lack of courage when faced with her father's disapproval. Ran had gone from her life when she'd betrayed him, and she'd accepted that—so to come suddenly face to face with him was a heart-wrenching shock. . .

LORD OF THE FOREST

Cal hoped arduous fieldwork in the Central American rain forest might salve her wounded heart. But it wasn't only the beauty of the forest that brought her joy and despair, for she'd reckoned without the fascination of Luis Revilla, the landowner who seemed determined to thwart her ideals. . .

LOVE'S AWAKENING

Selina had been just sixteen when she'd been emotionally blackmailed into marrying her Greek second cousin, Alex Petrides, and she'd run away within hours of the wedding, unable to face the night that would follow. She'd always expected Alex to follow her, but he hadn't, and now, three years later, something was calling her irresistibly back to Greece. . .

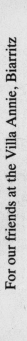

For our friends at the Villa Annie, Biarritz

CHAPTER ONE

OUTSIDE, the rain had stopped. The stone steps leading up to the church were steaming gently in the sun and, after the dim candlit interior, the brilliant sunlight of the Biarritz July afternoon was almost like a physical blow.

Jassy took a deep breath, not only to clear her lungs of the cloying atmosphere of lilies and incense, but also to overcome yet again that tight, choked feeling which, ever since Armand's death, had threatened to get the upper hand. All this vitality—the car horns on the Boulevard Leclerc, the yachts and windsurfers out at sea, a swirl of pigeons over the Place Saint Eugénie, the laughter and clink of wine glasses from the open window of La Baleine Bleue opposite—it all seemed incongruous, cruel even, when the old man, so vital, so life-loving in spite of his debilitating illness, was gone forever from the scene. . . .

She blinked back her tears, then turned to meet the sardonic gaze of the man who had just emerged from the porch. He had been sitting at the front of the church among the rest of the family, almost screened from her by one of the pillars. She'd only seen the back of his head, but there had been—something. And now, seeing him full face, she thought, Of course—Armand, forty years younger.

True, this man's face was unwrinkled, his hair

7

black, not grey, but the lean, hard features, the arrogant set of the head on the square shoulders were unmistakable. He must be Alain, Armand's nephew, flown in from New York, where he was in charge of the North American wing of the family empire. Over someone's shoulder she caught those steel-grey eyes again, held the look just for a moment, then her own slid away in confusion. Beneath Armand Deville's hard exterior had lurked a softness—for her, at any rate. But this man did not look as though he had an ounce of softness in his entire body—for anyone.

Behind her, the rest of the family—or pack, as Armand had privately referred to them—were spilling out, the men in formal dark suits, the women in chic black, each giving a cold eye one more obligatory dab with the obligatory black lace-edged handkerchief. Jassy caught again the potent whiffs of Milady, the flagship of the Deville perfumery which all the women seemed to have liberally coated themselves with—in a farewell gesture, presumably, to the founder of the family enterprise. What hypocrisy! Deep down below her grief, she felt anger stir, and turned away, tight-lipped.

Alongside this ostentatious show of wealth, she felt all at once out of place in her simple white blouse and straight navy linen skirt, and as the line of grey limousines drew silently up at the foot of the steps she drew back a little. Perhaps she would slip away now, unnoticed.

'Mademoiselle Powers!'

She swung round and recognised the plump figure of Marcel Ridoux, the Deville family lawyer, who had paid several visits to the Villa Chantal over the past few weeks.

'Monsieur Ridoux.' She smiled and they shook hands briefly.

'You are going to the cemetery, *mademoiselle*?'

'No, I don't think so. I wouldn't really have come, but Monsieur Deville has been so kind to me——' For a moment her voice trembled. 'I'll wait until the cars have gone, then go back to the villa and finish packing my things. After all, the family will no doubt want me out as soon as possible, if not before.'

But he returned her wry look with a decisive shake of the head. '*Non*, Mademoiselle Powers. Because you are a young woman who I am sure will always wish to behave correctly, you will accompany me to the cemetery, and then we shall follow the family back to the Villa Chantal.'

'Oh, I really don't——'

But the lawyer had already put a surprisingly firm grip on her elbow and was steering her in the direction of a black Peugeot.

'. . .and to Maurice Lavalle, my faithful and long-suffering valet, an annuity of. . .'

Monsieur Ridoux's precise voice droned on, and Jassy smothered a faint sigh. It was hot in the dining-room, even with all the tall windows thrown open to the terrace, and, finding that her attention had wandered yet again, she furtively straightened herself in her chair. Then, glancing up, she caught yet again those grey eyes of the man facing her and thrust down the feeling of growing irritation. She had, as she had thought, slipped into the room last, only to find him suddenly hard on her heels and sliding into the chair opposite.

She made herself return his cool glance with a frigid stare of her own and then, an instant before her composure began to crack, let her eyes slowly leave his and travel down the length of the polished table. Even so, her pulses were not quite steady and she knew that he must have seen the faint tinge of colour which, in spite of all her efforts, had crept into her cheeks.

Oh, why had Monsieur Ridoux insisted on prolonging her ordeal? When they had returned to the villa, tagging on to the convoy of limousines, instead of releasing her to go up to her room unseen, he had more or less frogmarched her into the reception-room, where Céline, the housekeeper, had prepared a light buffet meal.

True, once inside, with no hope of escape, he had allowed her to retreat to a far corner where, feeling distinctly fish-out-of-waterish, like Jane Eyre on the evening of Mr Rochester's dinner party, she had picked at a delicious, light-as-air, vol-au-vent and drunk the tea which one of the maids had brought her.

The others, of course, had all been knocking back the wine at a great rate and attacking the food with avidity. Oh, Armand, she had thought suddenly, if you could see them all now! But of course, he would only have quirked that eyebrow and flashed her a wickedly sardonic grin.

Only Alain Deville—it *was* him; she'd heard someone address him by name as they left the cemetery—seemed to have little appetite, and sat, absently revolving his wine glass on its fragile base and tapping his fingers against it, no doubt in a small private gesture of impatience, as he was engaged in conversation by Monique Deville, Armand's sister-in-law, and her daughter Martine. Those long, slender brown fingers. Jassy had been staring at them, as though hypnotised, when the movement stopped abruptly and she looked up to catch his watchful, faintly ironic gaze on her yet again.

When she had been drawn reluctantly into the room, the rest of the family had looked merely askance or, in the case of Monique, dagger-sharp. He, though, had raised his dark brows questioningly at Monsieur Ridoux and when the lawyer had returned his look with a professional blandness he had glanced back at her, his eyes narrowing just for an instant in what looked like a flicker of suspicion. . .

Jassy forced her attention back to the will. Armand's chauffeur, his gardener, old friends from those far-off days as a silent-film director, his doctor 'in forgiveness for the appalling régime he has enforced on me'—no one seemed to have been forgotten. A generous bequest to his housekeeper, Céline, and to each of the maids——

Oh, no! An appalling thought flashed into her mind. He hadn't left her anything, had he? Please, no, she prayed silently—it would be too embarrassing. As Armand's private physiotherapist she had been very well paid—he'd been a generous employer—and she had only been with him for six months. But he had. Suddenly, she knew that he had—only that would explain why Monsieur Ridoux had so insisted on her being present. . .

'. . .and to Jacinth Elizabeth Powers——' Jassy's hands clenched themselves in her lap '—I hope she will not object to my referring to her as a dear friend, for over the too few months I have known her I have come to appreciate and value the gentleness, patience and kindness she has unfailingly shown to a short-tempered old man——' she looked down, biting her lip against the tears '—with the exception of my personal effects already detailed, which my valet Maurice is to receive, I bequeath the Villa Chantal——'

'No—that's impossible!'

Jassy's shaking voice broke through the outraged gasp that had greeted the lawyer's words. She half raised herself from her chair, then sat down again— or rather, collapsed, as her legs gave way under her.

'I-I can't—there must be some mistake, Monsieur Ridoux.'

She looked appealingly at the lawyer, but he shook his head, with a faint smile. 'No, mistake, *mademoiselle*, I assure you.'

'But there must be!' From across the table, Monique, her beautifully made-up face a dull red, shot Jassy a vicious look, then swung round on the lawyer. 'As I am the widow of dear Armand's brother, the villa was intended for me—I know it was. That little tramp——'

'There is absolutely no mistake. I assure you, *madame*,' Monsieur Ridoux's chill voice cut in swiftly. He bent over the bulky typescript, one plump finger tracing alone a line. '. . .the Villa Chantal and all its contents, in grateful thanks.'

'For making an old man truly happy, you mean, Marcel.'

The lazy drawl came from opposite her, but at first Jassy was still so shaken that she scarcely heard the words and certainly did not register their meaning. Only when someone further down the table gave an openly suggestive laugh did she swivel round. He was lounging back easily enough in his chair, his hands in his pockets, but the look he directed at her was wholly unambivalent. Sick anger exploded in her.

'H-how dare you say that?'

She pushed back her chair and stood up, shaking back her coppery curls in a fierce gesture.

'Oh, I dare, *mademoiselle*, I dare.'

That hateful drawl again, and Jassy, just holding on to her temper with an enormous effort of will, stared down at him. She almost shook with the desire to leap on him, but as her hands curled themselves into fists she forced back the furious retort. She would not allow this man—arrogant, unpleasant brute that he was—to get under her skin, but she could knock some of that sneering self-assurance from his face, and from the others' too.

She slid into her chair again. 'Thank you, Monsieur—Deville, isn't it?' When he nodded, she somehow assembled on her face a dazzling smile. 'You've just helped me to make up my mind.'

'Really?' He raised his brows in mocking enquiry.

'Yes. You see, I was about to refuse the bequest. Oh, yes——' as she caught the sneer of open disbelief on his handsome face '—whether you choose to believe me or not, it's true—on the grounds that Monsieur Armand paid me far too generously for my services when he was alive.'

'Oh, *ma chère mademoiselle*, you underestimate yourself, I am sure.'

She gave him one look which should have nailed him to the back of his chair, then went on, 'But I've changed my mind.' With a defiant little toss of the head, she turned to the lawyer, her eyes skating past all the hostile faces. 'Thank you, Monsieur Ridoux, I accept the legacy.'

'But it's preposterous! The villa——'

'Oh, never mind the bloody villa, Maman,' the young man sitting next to Monique cut in. 'What about the company shares?'

Maman. So that must be Robert, Armand's other nephew and Alain's cousin. And yet there was only the most superficial likeness: both men were tall, well-built, with jet-black hair, but while Robert, although younger—only in his late twenties, Jassy judged—was already running to seed, his waistline thick, his face and jowls heavy, Alain was—under her lashes she sneaked a furtive glance across the table, and as she did so he unbuttoned his jacket, slipped it off and slung it carelessly across the back of his chair—Alain was all taut muscle, not an ounce of fat on him, the clean, hard outline of his shoulders and chest clearly visible against the fine white cotton of his shirt.

His face too, though so like Robert's in the groundwork, had none of the grossness of the younger man's: thin, angular—ascetic, almost. All

he needed was a cowl and he'd be a perfect monk—
the sort who would have cheerfully burnt at the
stake anyone who crossed him if he'd lived five
centuries ago.

She stared at him, more openly now. It was one
way, at least, to try and calm the still whirling
maelstrom of her thoughts, and she was perfectly
safe, for all his attention was on the lawyer, only his
fingers flicking a gold pen back and forth between
his palms to reveal that, for all his relaxed demean-
our, he was tense. The finely arched black brows,
well-shaped though obviously much more accus-
tomed to registering cynical world-weariness than
any other emotion, the straight, long nose, the hard
grey eyes, the lashes so ridiculously long, like a
girl's, that they cast a line of dense shadow across
his high cheekbones. But the softening effect
stopped right there; the mouth, though beautifully
formed, carried an unmistakable hint of danger in
the taut line of the lips. Those lips. . .

Jassy, feeling the guilty flush steal over her cheeks,
tore her eyes away to concentrate, like the others,
on the lawyer again.

'. . .To my nephew Alain, who already owns nine
per cent of the company shares, a further twenty-
one per cent. . .'

. . .The villa's indoor pool—ideal for the thalassotherapy she had used with Armand. . . Perhaps she
would abandon her other plan, stay here and open a
private clinic. After all, Biarritz was so——

'. . .to Jacinth Powers, to whom, confident in her
good sense, I am more than happy to bequeath
them.'

Jassy had put her hands flat down against the table. Now, as she moved them jerkily, she saw against the polished rosewood the clammy imprint of two palms. She ran the tip of her tongue around her dry lips and tried to swallow the saliva which was almost choking her.

'Is—it—a—joke?' She spoke very slowly, her brain stunned beyond coherent thought.

'No joke, Mademoiselle Powers.' The lawyer began briskly shuffling the papers into his briefcase.

'But it must be!' Monique had finally found her voice. She turned on another man, sitting towards the end of the table—Louis, an elderly cousin of Armand. He had at least been to see the old man fairly regularly and was so lacking in character as to be quite harmless. 'Why don't you say something, Louis? My God, if I were a man——'

'You would be a credit to your sex, Tante Monique.' Alain Deville's languid drawl broke in, but when Jassy looked across at him she saw that he too, despite having himself ruthlessly under control, was angry—no, not angry—furious. Her stomach gave a tremendous lurch of fear, and that unpleasant spasm roused her from her stupefaction.

Before she could speak, though, he was saying, 'Don't go just yet, Marcel. I want to clarify the main points of that document you are so busily removing—just so that we can all be quite certain of where we stand in this new situation.'

Jassy realised that, without raising his voice, he had somehow taken control of the room.

'To deal with the allotment of the Parfumerie Deville shares: one,' he touched one finger lightly with the other hand, 'my uncle had retained fifty-one per cent—giving him a controlling interest in the business. Two, I was given nine per cent when I came of age, and I am now to receive an additional twenty-one per cent. Three, the remaining forty per cent, divided equally between Tante Monique, her two children and Cousin Louis, remain un-changed——'

'Of course they do. We all heard him, didn't we?'

But ignoring his aunt's furious interruption, he went on in the same expressionless tone, 'Four, Mademoiselle Powers,' he did not even glance in her direction, 'is to receive the remaining thirty per cent, which means, unless my mathematics are failing me, that she and I now hold an equal thirty per cent each.'

His voice was still coldly dispassionate, as though he were analysing the day's weather. 'And she will also, I assume, take my uncle's place on the board.'

He looked enquiringly at Monsieur Ridoux, who nodded. 'That is perfectly correct, Monsieur Alain. With the rider that, in view of Mademoiselle's inexperience in business matters, you are to be Chairman and Managing Director——'

'Well, that's some small comfort, I suppose,' Monique broke in again. 'But it's an absolute dis-grace—and, Ridoux, you should have stopped the silly old fool. We shall contest it, of course. He must have been senile, so——'

'Far be it from me, as a lawyer, to advise you, *madame*, against going to litigation, but I feel I should warn you that I would have to give it as my personal assessment that Monsieur Deville was in full control of his faculties, not only when this will,' he gestured towards his briefcase, 'was made a month ago, but right up to the time of his death.'

Monique leaned forward, favouring Jassy with an evil look, then remarked to the room at large, 'I knew it all along. We should have got rid of her—like all the other little whores we've had to separate him from.'

'Perhaps I should point out,' the lawyer put in crisply, 'that Mademoiselle Powers knew absolutely nothing of the will—and, Madame Deville, I would beg you to remember that she speaks excellent French.'

The woman shrugged her plump shoulders in an ugly gesture. '*Tant pis.*'

'Anyway, Maman,' Robert chipped in, 'I somehow think you wouldn't have got rid of this one quite so easily. Armand seems to have been very—taken with her.'

Jassy winced inwardly at the snide innuendo in his voice, but somehow she forced herself to sit perfectly still, her hands clenched, her eyes grimly fixed on a point on the opposite wall.

She heard Monique snort. 'She must have been offering quite something, the little——'

Jassy did not know the word, but its meaning was unmistakable.

'That is enough, Tante Monique. You are beside yourself.'

Alain Deville had not raised his voice a quarter of a decibel, but his aunt's shrill tones stopped dead in mid-flow and with an angry—though silent—toss of the head, she began fumbling for the crocodile-skin bag at her feet.

Monsieur Ridoux was the last to leave. He came and stood beside Jassy, a faint smile on his face.

'Well, *mademoiselle*, so now you know why it was so imperative that you should be present.'

She gave him a wan smile. 'Yes. It—it's like a dream—although,' she pulled a face, 'just at this moment, I'm not sure whether it's a dream or a nightmare! An hour ago, I was wondering how long they'd give me to get packed up and now—well, I'm still frightened to death, of course. I don't know a thing about big business.' She took a shuddering breath, then looked straight at him. 'I meant what I said, you know. I *was* going to refuse the bequest. I still don't think it's right. I know none of them had been near him, until it was nearly too late, but even so——'

The horrified alarm of the lawyer who sensed a carefully constructed document falling apart before his eyes showed on his normally bland face—and, just for an instant, something else, which she could not identify, then, 'But you have changed your mind, *n'est-ce pas, mademoiselle*?'

'Yes—yes, I have,' she said firmly, and heard him breathe out a faint hiss of relief. 'I suppose it's my stubborn streak. If they all hadn't been so—so foul,' she grimaced at the memory, 'I'd have given in, I think, but they managed to bring out the worst in me. And besides, if Monsieur Armand really did want me to have the villa and those shares. . .'

Her voice tailed away and he put a large hand on her arm.

'He really did want that, *mademoiselle*. As an old friend, I am not breaking confidence—he truly did want it to be this way.'

'Oh, well,' she gave a shaky laugh and jumped to her feet, 'in that case, let battle commence.'

A grave smile flickered across his features. 'As you say, let battle commence. You are an intelligent young woman. You will soon learn about the business affairs of a large company and, looking at you, *mademoiselle*, and remembering how highly Armand regarded you—dare I say that, in my opinion, Powers versus Deville will without doubt be a battle of the Titans.'

CHAPTER TWO

Jassy stood motionless on the steps, until the Peugeot had swept away out of sight down the long shady avenue of plane trees. Finally, hearing one of the servants moving about in the house, she went slowly back into the cool, dim hall.

Facing her was a huge gilded Louis Quinze mirror, and she stopped in front of it, frowning abstractedly at her reflection. . . Quite tall, slim, the simple blouse and straight skirt emphasising the high, full breasts, the slender waist and long curve of her hips. . . Those coppery curls tumbling to her shoulders and the slanting, brilliant green eyes— rather too catlike and penetrating for masculine comfort, most men seemed to decide, just before backing off in search of more—*pliable* young women. . . The delicate oval of her face, with its magnolia-pale complexion—and definitely more pale than magnolia just now, she decided, on closer inspection.

What you need is a stiff drink, my girl, she told herself, and went through into the dining-room, where she remembered seeing Louis and several of the other men fortifying themselves for the rigours of the will-reading with best Scotch whisky.

Yes, there were the bottles on a side table, two empty but one still half full. She poured herself a small measure, hesitated, added another more generous shot and picked up the tumbler.

'That's right. You can drop the demure little tea-drinker act now, Mademoiselle Powers.'

The glass almost leapt from her hand, the whisky jolting over her fingers and dribbling down on to the polished parquet floor. She spun round and saw Alain Deville lounging against the marble fireplace.

'I thought you'd gone,' she blurted out.

'Obviously—but no, *ma chère*. You see, I wanted a private word with you.'

As she stared at him, he straightened up and sauntered over to her. The anger was emanating from him in waves; she could almost see it, certainly feel it, and in spite of herself she took a step back, fetching up hard against the table.

'Don't you dare touch me!'

His lip curled contemptuously. 'Oh, so we have the shrinking violet act now, do we? Very convincing. But don't worry, *mademoiselle*, I would not care to dirty my hands on you.' Then, as she looked around the room for a way of escape, 'Or perhaps you intend to have some of *your* servants throw me out as an undesirable intruder?'

The savagery in his voice almost knocked the breath from her, but somehow she had to drag herself together. There could be no half measures here. Heaven knew, Monique Deville was viper-fanged enough, but, some feline instinct for self-preservation told her, with this man it would be fight or be trampled underfoot. Well, she wasn't going to just lie down submissively under anyone's chariot wheels!

Setting her small, neat chin at a determined angle, she said coolly, 'That, *monsieur*, depends entirely on you.'

'Hmm.' He studied her for long moments, his eyes narrowed but his face carefully wiped clear of any expression. Then, '*Enfin*, I suppose I should congratulate you, *mademoiselle*, on your good fortune. In the turmoil, we all omitted that simple politeness.'

Jassy looked quickly at him, but there was no clue to be read in his face. Perhaps, after all, with his quick intelligence, he had realised that for both of them a truce, albeit an armed one, would be preferable to open warfare, so she said guardedly, 'Thank you.'

'You have not been in Biarritz for very long, I believe?'

'Nearly a year.' Encouraged by his silence, she went on, 'I wanted to get experience in water physiotherapy, and as the thalassotherapy clinic here has such a great reputation, it was the obvious place to come. Then, when I met your uncle, he asked me to move to the villa to work privately for him, so——'

'You must be an extremely skilful young woman.'

'Well, I hope so, *monsieur*. You see, I would like——'

'It did not take you long.'

There was—something in his voice, but those cool grey eyes were still completely unreadable.

'I—I don't know what you mean.'

'Oh, come now, *mademoiselle*. Grant me some intelligence. We understand each other perfectly, you and I. You came out here deliberately—what is

the word?—*prospecting*.' As she stared blankly at
him he added impatiently, so there should be no
mistake, 'Prospecting for a wealthy, susceptible old
man. And at your very first attempt, you struck
gold. Yes, Biarritz must have seemed like a new
Klondike to a cheap little gold-digger like you.'

Too sickened for anger, Jassy gasped and drew
back her head sharply, then bit fiercely on the soft
inner flesh in her mouth in an effort to suppress the
disgust that was rising in her throat.

Alain Deville put out his hand and, before she
could jerk away, tilted her face towards him, his
fingers digging cruelly into her flesh. He studied her
features in silence, but then his lips tightened and,
with a mirthless laugh, he abruptly released his hold.

'Well, Armand always did have a proverbial soft
spot for a pretty face, and I must admit, *mademoiselle*, that, though not to my personal taste, of
course, yours is quite something.'

The burning anger was welling up now, threatening to overflow, but she struggled desperately to
hold it in check. 'Your uncle was over eighty—a
very sick old man. If I thought for a minute you
were insinuating anything, I would——'

'You would, no doubt, have been quite prepared
to accommodate him. After all, surely seduction of
aged Romeos is a vital part of every gold-digger's
portfolio.'

'You filthy-minded devil!' With no conscious
thought, she brought her hand up, and before he
could step back out of range she had struck him full
on the face. It was a violent blow which, for a
moment, rocked him on his heels. As he put his

hand to his cheek, where the flesh first turned white, then red, she stared up at him, stormy-eyed, her breast heaving.

'Well, go on, then—hit me back! That's what you're longing to do, isn't it?'

'I am longing to do all sorts of things to you, *mademoiselle*, none of which you would find in the least pleasant, I assure you. My uncle——'

'No!' she burst out, her eyes spitting green fire. 'You can say what you like about me, think what you like, but I won't have you say one word about Monsieur Deville!' Another flash of green sparks. 'He was a brave old man, a true friend of mine, but as for anything m-more——' She broke off, struggling for composure.

'How old are you?' His eyes were like grey flint, but she saw with some small satisfaction the outline of her fingers raising a puffy, angry weal across his cheek.

'Twenty-seven. Not that it's anything to do with you.'

'Oh, I think you will find,' his voice was smooth—he had himself well under control again now, 'that everything to do with Mademoiselle Jacinth Elizabeth Powers is to do with me. Twenty-seven, and yet you have not married. Why is that, I wonder?'

'Does every woman have to? Does it offend your male love of neatness if any one of us is allowed to float around unattached?'

He shrugged. 'A simple question.'

'Well, let's just say I'm choosy, then. Mr Right hasn't happened to cross my path yet.'

'And would you recognise him if he did?'

'Oh, I think so.' And he wouldn't be six feet of infuriatingly arrogant overbearing Frenchman, for a start!

'But you are still looking?'

'No, I'm not!' she flared. 'For your information, I'm perfectly happy as I am—footloose and fancy free.' She took a deep breath in an effort to recover her tattered poise. 'Now, if you'll excuse me, I've a great deal to see to.'

'But of course.' He eyed her evenly. 'Although you must already have given the matter of your so unexpected windfall considerable thought. It is ironic, *n'est-ce pas*? If you had picked my pocket of a hundred francs, I could hand you over to the gendarmerie——'

'Yes, and wouldn't you just enjoy doing it? No doubt you'd be only sorry that the days of the thumbscrew have gone—they *have* gone in France, I presume?'

'—but as it is, I can do nothing. I have been tied—we all have—hand and foot, by knots which are completely legal, and there is no escape.'

Jassy heard, beneath the anger, the frustration in his voice. On any other occasion, she would have been sorry—sorry to have caused so much trouble and upset to a family, however appalling that family might be, but, she told herself fiercely, she was glad—glad—glad! It was time this family as a whole, and one member in particular, had a spoke put in its unpleasant, arrogant wheel.

So she said, in a honey tone, 'I suppose, *monsieur*, you think your uncle should have bequeathed the lot—the villa, its contents, all his shares—to you.'

She returned his angry scowl with a sweet smile. 'After all, you and the rest of your charming relatives have such a strong sense of family obligation.'

'For the others—that is their affair, but I, as a matter of fact, do have such a strong sense that I gave up the running of my own electronics company and have spent the last few months working abroad, first in Japan and then in the States, often for sixteen hours a day, to try to pull Deville through some grave financial difficulties. You will not have known about them, *mademoiselle*. I took good care to keep my problems from Armand. I didn't want his health to be put further at risk by any business worries.'

'I think,' she said more gently, 'that he had a pretty good idea.' Then as she saw a fleeting hint of pain in his grey eyes, she added swiftly, 'But it made no difference, I promise you. He was past worrying about the company by then, so you really mustn't reproach yourself.'

Driven by some impulse to reach out to him, she went to put a hand on his arm, but then, at the forbidding expression in his eyes, she let it drop to her side again and merely added formally, 'I hope your efforts were successful.'

'Why? Are you afraid, perhaps, that the value of your hard-earned booty is slipping away already?'

Oh, what was the use? 'No, I'm not, damn you! I don't care that much,' she snapped her fingers in his face, 'for your stupid shares.'

'Please.' He held up a hand to silence her. 'No more. We are only wasting time.'

He sat down at the table, took out his chequebook, laid it in front of him, then unscrewed his gold fountain pen. Finally he looked up at her. 'Your price, *mademoiselle*?'

'My——?' Jassy gaped at him, puzzled.

'Your price.' He tapped the pen impatiently against the cheque-book. 'You must have one—every woman does.'

'For what?' What game was he playing with her now?

'For your shares, of course.'

So that was it. He really did think that she was such a cheap little on-the-make that she could, at a cost, be bought off. Righteous anger rose inside her in a boiling tide, and with it came the intense desire to fall on him as he sat, so cool, so—bloody arrogant, at the table there, and rend him limb from well-built limb. But with this man any violence on her part would, she was sure, be more than equally repaid. So—softly, softly. . .

'My—price? What exactly did you have in mind?'

He gave her a long look, then said slowly, 'So you're determined to milk the company for every centime you can get. I underestimated you. I thought that a fat wad of banknotes in that slim little hand of yours would be preferable to any bird in the bush, as it were.'

He sat back, his fingertips together, studying her over the arch of his hands. 'So, tell me. You must have some real ambition—you look to me an extremely ambitious young woman, and you surely did not intend to remain a—masseuse——' he made the word an open insult '—forever.'

'For your information, I am not a masseuse—or,

at least, only partly. I'm a fully qualified physiotherapist.'

Her pipe-dream, to one day have her very own health hydro, was hovering on the very tip of her tongue, but to let him know that would merely confirm his blackest suspicions of her. So instead, she took a deep breath.

'Monsieur Deville, I swear to you that until this afternoon I knew nothing about the bequest——'

'Oh, please, spare me. A member of the family had already been in touch with me,' oh, yes, and I wonder who that could have been? she thought bitterly, 'to say that in their opinion you were obtaining far too much influence over him.'

'Well, I don't see how they could have known that,' she burst out hotly. 'They never came near him—none of them. You won't believe me, I know, if I say it a million times, but I was very fond of your uncle. No,' she went on more softly, 'I loved him. He—he was like the grandfather I never knew.'

'However, I ignored the warning——' What was wrong with him, for heaven's sake? Didn't he ever listen to anything anyone said?

His eyes skimmed over her in a leisurely perusal which was so frankly sexual that she put her arms to her breasts in a reflex protective gesture.

'—wrongly, I now know—now that it is too late.'

He flicked back his jacket sleeve to look at his watch, then gave an irritable exclamation. 'For the final time, how much will you take for the shares?'

Jassy gazed past him out of the window unseeingly. She didn't care a snap for the other Devilles' opinion of her, and yet, for some unaccountable reason, she suddenly knew that she cared very deeply what he thought of her. Oh, well. She gave a tiny rueful shrug. He'd made up his mind that she was a tough, granite-hearted bitch, and nothing would shift him. Well, all right, if that was what he chose to believe, that was what she would have to be.

She walked across to him, deliberately increasing the slight natural sway of her hips, and leaned against the table-edge, her thigh all but touching his arm. Infusing her green eyes with what she hoped was a smouldering languor, she stared down at him, then, as she noted with satisfaction the faint colour creep along his cheekbones and the quickening rise and fall of his chest, she said huskily, 'You know the swimming-pool outside?'

He frowned, temporarily thrown off balance, then nodded.

'Well, go and jump in it!' she yelled, right in his face. 'Preferably with all your clothes on and a five-ton weight tied to your ankles!'

As he leapt to his feet, she hurled at him, only slightly less loudly, 'I don't want those loathsome shares, but your uncle wanted me to have them, and after all the things you've said to me today, calling me everything but a whore—and you didn't need to do that, your precious aunt did it for you—well, you can just go to hell, the lot of you. I'm keeping them, and there's not a damn thing you can do about it!'

He muttered something in gutter French, then with a furious gesture swept up his cheque-book and pen, jamming them into his inside pocket. He stood regarding her with a thunderous scowl.

'When Ridoux left just now, he wished me luck. I see now what the old devil meant. You, *mademoiselle*, are the most *insupportable* young woman it has ever been my misfortune to encounter!'

With no warning at all, Jassy's anger evaporated and hot tears came burning into her eyes. 'Oh, you look just like Armand.' In spite of herself, it burst out, and she gave him a blurred smile. 'When we were arguing, when I was trying to get him to do some particularly unpleasant water therapy on that knee of his, he'd look at me just like that, as if I were a nasty smell just under his aristocratic nose.' She shook her head, unable to continue.

'Tears? How affecting,' he drawled.

A wave of sadness engulfed her, but she forced a careless shrug. 'You must think what you like of me, Monsieur Deville. Oh, just one other thing.'

He was walking towards the door, but stopped and turned back, his brows raised impatiently. 'Yes?'

'Those water exercises. However much he fought me—in the end, Armand always *did* do them.'

Their glances held for a moment, then he swung on his heel and walked out of the room.

Jassy reached over to clip a last Reine Victoria rose, which she had told Céline she would pick for the cut-glass bowl in the hall, then, burying her nose luxuriously in the pink honey-sweet globes, she wandered across to the terrace and perched on the low stone wall beside the swimming-pool.

She let her eyes drift across its pale blue, unruffled surface to the house beyond. Am I dreaming? Is all this really happening to me? She had asked herself this each morning when she'd woken, and a thousand times during the last two days, and still could not quite believe it, still had the urge to pinch herself very hard.

This beautiful villa, in the elegant *fin-de-siècle* style of grey, Virginia-creepered stone, dove-grey shutters, misty blue roof slates. . .the well-tended grounds, bounded around the perimeter by a thick belt of mature trees. . .the long sweep of gravelled drive, lined with pleached plane trees and underplanted with hydrangeas, their blue lacy heads as big as dinner plates. . . Was it all hers?

Incredibly, yes. And soon she was going to have to take some decisions over her future. She sighed faintly, watching her toe absently trace round a crack in the paving stone. By far the easiest thing would be to submit gracefully to Alain Deville's wishes: sell him her shares, at a fair market price—ill-mannered brute though he was, she wasn't in the business of running an extortion racket—then sell the villa and return home.

Surely she'd raise enough to buy a country house in England suitable for that health hydro she had so long dreamed of. Perhaps near London would be sensible—lots of over-stressed City types crying out for a few days' pampering. . .

Céline was gesturing urgently to her from one of the french windows. She picked up the basket of roses and went across to her.

'Oh, Mademoiselle Jacinth,' the housekeeper was flustered, 'I didn't know what to do. It's Monsieur Alain on the telephone——'

'But I told you, if he rang, to say that I was out.'

'I know, *mademoiselle*, but he says that he knows you are in and will just keep on until you do speak to him.'

Jassy strongly suspected that, given Alain Deville's dubious temper, she was receiving a highly censored version of his message.

'Thank you, Céline,' she said tightly, 'I'll speak to him—and please don't worry.'

She gave the housekeeper a reassuring smile, handed the roses to her and watched her disappear down the passage. Through the open door, she glimpsed the phone off the hook in the living-room. What did he want? Almost certain that he would not take no for an answer, she'd given Céline her instructions, but in fact there had been a heavy silence for two days. She had told herself that he was still licking his wounds, but it was far more likely, she was sure, that he was plotting some new, devious strategy.

As she picked up the phone, the nervousness curled itself like cold fingers around her stomach.

'J-Jacinth Powers here.'

'Ah, so pleased that you are in, after all.'

The faint irony grated on her like sandpaper rasped over her nerve-ends and she said abruptly, 'If you're ringing about the shares, you can forget it.'

'By all means, if you say so, *mademoiselle*.' Still that faint irony. 'But I do have a proposition to put to you which I trust you will find of interest.'

'Oh?' She couldn't quite keep the suspicion from her voice, and she heard him give a slight laugh.

'Don't worry. I think you'll find that it is as much to your benefit as mine.'

What a lovely voice he had when he wasn't hurling abuse at her! Deep and husky, it was sending pleasant if highly disturbing little vibrations down through her left eardrum to every part of her body. . .

'Shall we say in half an hour?'

'What? Can't you tell me over the phone?'

'I would rather not. So I'll call round—if that is quite convenient, of course.' And it had better be, was the clear if unspoken implication.

'Well, I-I'm not sure,' Jassy temporised hastily. Little pig, little pig, let me come in. Was it altogether wise to fling open her front door to this particular wolf?

'Right—in half an hour, then?' Or I'll huff and I'll puff and I'll blow your house down.

She glanced at the ornate ormolu clock on the mantelpiece. 'Hold on a moment, please.' She riffled loudly through the blank pages of an appointments book on the shelf beside her, then said in her most formal tone, 'Yes, I find I have no appointment then. Eleven o'clock will be fine, Monsieur Deville.'

'I'm so glad, Mademoiselle Powers.' She could almost see that infuriating smile. 'I look forward to our meeting. *A tout à l'heure.*' And with a decisive click the phone went dead.

Jassy replaced the receiver, at the same time expelling her pent-up feelings in a low, slow breath, then sat staring down at the ivory and red lacquer firescreen in the empty grate. What did he want? A proposition. Well, no matter what he might say, one

thing was for sure—whatever there might be in it for
A Deville, there'd be nothing good for J Powers!

She caught sight of her misty reflection in one of
the polished lacquer panels and leapt to her feet
with a gasp of horror. She couldn't possibly receive
him like this! Earlier, she had been clearing out a
huge cupboard in the small, pretty room upstairs,
which had obviously once been a lady's boudoir—
perhaps for the very Chantal that the villa was
named after, the early movie star who had once
shared Armand's life before being killed in a tragic
car crash in the 1940s, and whom he had spoken of
with such nostalgic tenderness. Now, her jeans and
white T-shirt were festooned with dust and cobwebs,
and when she tugged off the old chiffon scarf from
her hair, a cloud of fine grey dust floated lazily into
the air.

She fled through the hall, then stopped at the foot
of the staircase, picking at the balustrade. Did it
matter what she wore to receive him? No, of course
not. She was on her own territory, wasn't she? And
besides, she'd always scorned to be one of those
women who dressed to please men. On the other
hand, facing Alain Deville in faded jeans and tatty
canvas espadrilles would be about as sensible as
confronting a marauding tiger with both hands tied
behind your back.

Up in her bedroom, she flung off her clothes, took
a speedy shower, hesitated in front of her wardrobe
for just one second, then pulled out a dress which
had been an impulse buy a couple of weeks before,
from a small boutique in the Rue du Port Vieux.
She stepped into it, pulled up the long zip, then

scrutinised herself, unable to resist a little nod of
satisfaction. The colour—a muted sage-green—set
off to perfection her flawless magnolia complexion
and mass of copper curls, intensifying the green of
her eyes, while the simple style enhanced her slender
figure, the fine cotton jersey clinging to her like a
second skin down to hip level, then flaring into a
slight bias-cut swirl, so that as she moved it rippled
against her legs and thighs as though she were gliding
through water.

She thrust her feet into white patent pumps.
Ouch—they were so tight she couldn't even wriggle
her toes. For months, she had virtually lived in
sandals or espadrilles, and now her feet were definitely half a size broader. But she sternly resisted
the temptation to climb back into her espadrilles—
after all, she only had to walk gracefully to the
nearest chair.

A hasty dab of perfume behind her ears, a rapid
application of pale coral gloss to her wide, full
mouth, a frenzied but wholly unsuccessful attempt
with her Afro comb to subdue her curls into chic,
soignéed order, and then she made her way gingerly
downstairs. She was just crossing the hall when
simultaneously the ormolu clock tinkled eleven and
an imperious finger jabbed long and hard on the
doorbell.

'It's all right, Céline. I'll get it.'

And without giving herself time to surrender to
those treacherous butterflies of panic which were
rustling around somewhere below her ribs, Jassy
tacked an insincere smile firmly into place and
opened the door.

CHAPTER THREE

ALAIN DEVILLE had been standing with his back to her, surveying the garden—no doubt mourning the loss of a fine piece of real estate, Jassy told herself sardonically, but then as he swung round she smothered the uncharitable thought.

'Good morning, Monsieur Deville.' Her tone, though frosty, was polite—just.

'Good morning—again, Mademoiselle Powers.' Still that faintly ironic note. He thrust a huge, lavishly beribboned bouquet at her.

'Oh, thank you, they're b-beautiful.'

Caught completely off guard, Jassy heard herself stammering and bent her head hastily to sniff at the sweet-scented pink rose-peonies, big as cabbage hearts, the blue and white irises, and marguerites.

'But why?' She eyed him warily.

He shrugged. 'Do I need a reason?' But then he slanted her an unashamedly wicked smile. 'However, if you wish, a small peace-offering.'

Across the fragile barrier of petals, their gazes held for a moment before hers slid away. All her suspicions were aroused and she was tempted to push the flowers back at him and retreat inside, but she knew that would only be a fatal sign of weakness, so instead she opened the door a fraction wider.

'Please come in.'

When she entered the sitting-room from handing

the flowers over to Céline, he was sprawled back on the sofa, one arm casually behind his head, and she was very conscious of his eyes on her, frankly taking in the lines of her body beneath the clinging jersey dress. For a second, she wished that she'd stayed with the jeans and T-shirt, but no—he saw her as an old-fashioned vamp and she would hate to spoil his image of her.

She felt unaccountably nervous under his cool scrutiny, though, so to still the tremors she said, 'Would you like a drink?' gesturing towards a side table where some of the bottles, including the whisky, still stood untouched since the funeral.

'No, thank you, it's a little early in the day for me. But don't let me stop you.'

The clear implication in his voice caught her on the raw. 'I rarely drink, and never whisky,' she snapped. 'That day, if you recall, I'd had several shocks in quick succession. Now, I'm extremely busy, Monsieur Deville. What do you want?'

He sighed extravagantly. 'Oh, dear! I was hoping our last encounter was an aberration, and you were not invariably a sharp-tongued little termagant.'

'Well, you should recognise the breed. There are enough of them in your family,' she retorted.

But he only smiled, a rather feline smile. 'However, I begin to fear that it is your natural disposition.'

It was happening all over again—here he was, lounging back, quite at his ease, and straight away getting under several layers of her skin. Jassy realised that she was still standing by the table, and sank down into the nearest chair, her hands clenched tightly in her lap.

'Shall I tell you something, Monsieur Deville?'

He pulled a face. 'Please, Alain. I think you and I have gone well past the stage of formality—Jassy.'

'My name, Monsieur Deville, is Jacinth,' she said tightly, then after a pause added, 'I am only Jassy to my very closest friends.'

But still she didn't seem able to get through to him, needle him. He only spread his hands in a mock-surrender gesture and leaned back, his eyes glinting as though he were enjoying a secret joke which she was quite sure she would not want to share. She stared at him, perplexed. Somehow, without his moving a muscle, raising his voice in the least, she could feel the initiative—if she'd ever had it—moving out of her grasp as, gently but inexorably, he reeled her in as though she were a fish on a line. She sat up a little straighter in her chair.

'I really would have sold those shares to you, you know. I don't know anything about business, and I do want to get back to physiotherapy. I'm thinking of turning the villa into a clinic, so——'

'If you do that, you're a fool.'

'And what do you mean by that?' she demanded belligerently.

'Just this. Tonight, take off those ridiculous shoes that you can hardly walk in and have a stroll around the town, making a note of all the brass plates you see. Among all the rheumatologists, cardiologists and all the other ologists, I can tell you you will find more than sufficient long-established physiotherapists and masseurs.'

Jassy stared at him, biting her underlip. He was right, of course. Subconsciously, she had known all along—it was just a futile dream. But she was not going to let him see that he had succeeded in undermining her, so, ignoring his words, she went on haughtily, 'I would have let you have them, but men like you bring out the worst in me, so I'm not——'

'And what sort of men,' he let his eyes wander in a lazy trail over her face and body in what was nothing less than a physical assault, so that she drew back instinctively into the safety of the upholstered chair, feeling her pulses flicker in alarm, 'or rather, what sort of a man, I ask myself, would bring out the *best* in you? What——' softly, as she coloured in silent, angry confusion '——no response from that ever-ready tongue of yours?'

He paused, scrutinising her face for a moment, then, as though satisfied with the effect of his words, 'But in any case, I am afraid that I am not here to waste my valuable time making you another generous offer which you would no doubt, out of sheer malice, fling back in my face.'

'Oh?'

She was almost disappointed—and more than a little disturbed. If she'd sold him the shares, she would never have had to face him again. On the other hand, if she was going to retain them, she would presumably, as a member of the Deville board, be in constant proximity to him, and she was not at all sure that she found that idea very appealing. . .

She shot him a quick glance. He was dressed

casually enough, in pale grey lightweight trousers and a short-sleeved lemon cotton shirt, the open neck revealing the strong column of his tanned throat, a tiny sprinkling of fine dark hair just visible in the V, but still, lounging back almost languidly, he emanated power both of intellect and body.

All at once, in some strange way, Jassy was reminded of Armand's vintage Mercedes-Benz, which he had given to a motor museum a few weeks before he died. She had seen the highly charged vehicle pushed out on to the drive, to lie like a black cat basking in the sun. But then one of the mechanics had switched on, and instantly the huge engine had roared into life and the harmless cat had changed, before her eyes, into a menacing black panther.

Be careful, my girl, she thought suddenly, with a tiny flicker of fear. This one is dynamite. Lethal looks, lethal charm, no doubt, when he chooses—that 'peace-offering' of a bouquet—in fact, lethal, full stop.

And she didn't at all like the way he was still leaning back, one leg crossed negligently over the other, apparently engrossed in swinging the heel of his sandal to and fro, though she knew quite well that those penetrating grey eyes were not missing anything of what was going through her head.

'You said you have a proposition to put to me,' she prompted, and was angry when she heard her own voice, husky with uncertainty.

He stood up abruptly. 'It can wait. I'm taking you out—oh, don't look so suspicious, my dear Jassy——'

'Jacinth.'

'—I'm not planning on luring you to the nearest cliff——'

'No, but you'd like to,' she blurted out.

He shot her a white-toothed, shark—no, wolf smile. She really had let the wolf in over her doorstep.

'Well, perhaps—although it would be such a waste of that beautiful body of yours.'

Then, as she sat gaping up at him, like that fish, finally landed, he took her hand, and before she could even decide whether she was going with him or not she was somehow out of the chair and on her feet.

'I'm taking you to the industrial estate in Bayonne, where we have our factory. As you're a newly created major shareholder,' she made herself ignore the thrust, 'it's time you met our work-force—and we might even persuade you to forsake Mitsouko for one of our own excellent products.'

Jassy gave a start—he'd obviously been subjecting her to an even closer scrutiny than she'd realised—but then she relaxed slightly. After all, awareness of perfumes was presumably just a mundane part of his stock-in-trade, and therefore it was in fact no more than a reflex reaction on his part.

'Strange,' he shook his head ruminatively as he gestured her past him, 'that a woman apparently composed entirely of granite, flint and acid should favour such a feminine, seductive, *sensual* perfume as Mitsouko.'

So he was obviously baiting her, after all, but she would not allow herself to respond. Instead she put her head in the air and walked past him out to the drive, where a steel-grey Citroën 25 Turbo was parked. As he handed her in, she gave the windscreen wipers her rapt attention and continued to ignore him as he slid in beside her, though her mind was racing.

What was he up to? They'd only met twice, but each time she'd dared to cross swords with him, and she knew enough about the Deville males to be sure that they did not care for that, particularly from a woman.

As he negotiated the big car out into the late morning traffic, she sneaked a sideways look at him. His austere face was composed in an almost amiable expression, although his mouth surely was still a firm, tightly held line. Yes, that mouth betrayed him. Behind the handsome forehead, some devious plot was definitely being hatched—and equally definitely, that plot intimately concerned her.

'And this is where the maturing process takes place.'

Alain Deville ushered Jassy into a long, dimly lit room. She was panting slightly from the effort of keeping up with him on what was turning out to be a whirlwind tour of the entire perfume-making operation, and the chill air made goose-bumps rise on her skin.

'All these——' she gestured to several rows of tall stainless-steel tanks stretching away into the gloom '—have they got perfume in them?'

'That's right.' He patted the nearest tank. 'It stays in these for a year. Each one can hold five hundred litres, enough perfume to fill sixteen thousand thirty-millilitre bottles.'

'Good grief!' Jassy gave a low whistle of astonishment. 'Sixteen *thousand*?'

'Yes—and there are fifty tanks in here.'

She moved slowly on down the row, peering at the labels.

'Oh, this one's Milady.'

'Yes—not to your taste, I think,' he said drily.

She had not heard him come up behind her, and when she felt his warm breath on her neck she stepped back too quickly in the confined space, only managing to collide sharply with his hard body. She turned to apologise, but then, finding herself staring up into his eyes from a distance of a few inches, moved back again, to jolt her elbow against the Milady container.

'And th-this next one,' she turned away quickly and became very interested in the label, 'oh yes, Field Sports—that's one of your new colognes for men, isn't it?'

'That's right. At least you know your house names.'

He was alongside her again, blocking her escape, and now, at the end of one of the rows, there was simply nowhere else for her to retreat to.

'Well, Armand talked to me a lot about them.'

Her voice sounded really shaky, she thought with intense exasperation—almost as though she were frightened of him, for heaven's sake—but then, as she took a deep breath, he at last stepped back to allow her past.

'Yes,' she went on, in something nearer her normal voice, 'he kept his interest in the firm right to the end, you know. When he first started to talk to me about it—how he founded the company with the money he'd made from his movies—I was interested, and after that—well, almost every day he would tell me more. Oh!' She stopped suddenly, then, as he looked at her enquiringly, forced herself to continue. 'I wonder if he'd already made up his mind to—well. . .' She floundered to a halt.

'To change his will in your favour, you mean?' His voice was bland. 'That, *ma chère* Jassy, is the very thing I was asking myself.'

They were suddenly on dangerous ground again and she needed to get off it. Her eyes roamed back to the containers.

'And what happens to the perfume at the end of a year?'

'It's cooled right down to one degree Centigrade, then filtered to make sure that it's absolutely clear.'

'And after that it's bottled?'

He nodded. 'Bottled, capped, labelled Deville, Biarritz and Paris, and within a week or two it's in New York, London, Tokyo—everywhere.'

Suddenly, without warning Jassy shivered violently. 'Ugh, it's cold in here!'

He rested his hand briefly on her arm.

'Yes, you're frozen. We've been in here long enough.'

But *his* hand was warm. The vibrant life was surging through it, and as they walked back towards the door she could still feel the imprint of his fingers, though not cooling—on the contrary, the heat from his hand seemed to be spreading all up her arm until the skin felt burning hot.

The only sound in the huge room was their

footsteps, echoing softly off the metal vats and, terrified that he would hear her heart, which had begun beating against her ribs in a rapid tattoo, she said loudly over her shoulder, 'This place isn't at all how I'd imagined it. It's all so—so clinical.'

'And what did you expect—hunched little figures crouching over enormous baskets of lavender and orange blossom, like something out of Charles Dickens?'

'Well, yes, I suppose I did.' She gave a slightly shamefaced laugh.

He pushed open the door for her. 'Now, let's have that thing.'

Jassy unbuttoned the long white overall and handed it to him. He hung it on a nearby hook, then turned back to her, and, before she could move, had adroitly untied the white square which was covering her hair and twitched it away so that her copper curls tumbled on to her shoulders.

Automatically, she put up both hands to smooth them down, but then, as she caught Alain Deville's eye, her hands stilled. He was staring at her with something very like shock in his eyes and his expression all at once made her breath catch in her throat again. For endless moments, the look held, then simultaneously, it seemed, as though feeling the need to break free, they both took a step backwards away from each other.

He half turned to begin unbuttoning his own overall and Jassy, still more than a little under the influence of the expression in those grey eyes, found herself babbling, 'All you need is a face mask and you'd make a perfect surgeon.'

He tugged off the white cap and tossed it on to the peg.

'What you mean, of course, is that you can just imagine me wielding a razor-sharp scalpel.' His voice seemed completely under control, but he still did not quite look at her.

'Well, since you mention it, yes, perfectly.'

He pulled a wry face. 'Hmm. Well, I shall take it as a compliment, though I doubt that was how you intended it.'

'But of course I did.' Grateful that the tension had eased, she even managed to shoot him a demure look from under her lashes.

'Of course,' he nodded, deadpan. 'Now, let's have a look at the laboratory.'

As she followed him into a large, well-lit room, Jassy was thinking, almost with alarm, Whatever's happening? We've been together for well over an hour and we've actually managed not to come to blows, or even to a snarling match, in all that time. She shook her head to try to clear it of the fog of bewilderment and moved towards the middle-aged man who was sitting at one of the benches, littered with dozens of glass jars and rods in wooden racks.

'Michel, I'd like you to meet Jacinth Powers, who has recently joined us. Jacinth, Michel Dupont.' As Jassy took the man's hand, Alain Deville went on, 'Michel is our *parfumeur*. He—or rather, that nose of his,' he grinned at the other man, 'is the most important member of our team. We still blend our own perfumes and don't buy them in—unlike most perfume houses today.'

'*Enchanté,* Mademoiselle Powers.'

The chemist bent over her hand in a gallant gesture, but the look he sent her was shrewd enough, and there was that same feeling of intense curiosity, of being thoroughly appraised, which her intuition had picked up from all the individuals she had met in the last hour. So the story of her sudden arrival on the scene was common knowledge, she thought ruefully—but after all, how could it be otherwise? She wondered what they all made of her—certainly Michel Dupont was looking faintly 'surprised, as though he'd expected her to have two heads, at least.

'I'm so pleased to meet you, Monsieur Dupont.'

She gave him a radiant smile, which seemed to almost knock him off his feet, then as she turned to Alain Deville, who had been watching the scene, she caught the faintest quirk of amusement at one corner of his thin mouth. She treated that secret little smile to a cool look, then turned back to the chemist.

'Monsieur Deville has been telling me all about the flower oils you keep in here.'

'Ah yes, *mademoiselle*, I shall be most happy to——'

But Alain Deville put a firm hand on his arm. 'Don't let us interrupt you, Michel. I will give Mademoiselle Powers her tour of inspection.'

He led her to the far end of the room, where row upon row of bottles lined the shelves and, running his finger along them, he picked out a large brown one. He uncorked it very carefully, then held it to her nose for her to take a deep sniff.

'Natural jasmine extract.'

'Mmm—wonderful. Oh, but it's so strong!' She drew back with a gasp, then, as he recorked the bottle, 'Do you realise that's the first actual smell of anything like a perfume that I've had since we arrived?'

He laughed. 'Well, perfume's too precious to scatter to the winds. We keep it very carefully under wraps.' He held the bottle up, tilting it slowly for her from side to side. 'How much do you think this jasmine absolute is worth?'

'Oh, I've no idea.'

'On the world market now it costs at least sixty thousand francs a kilo, so this bottle would be about forty thousand.' He gave her a sly smile and held it out to her. 'Another sniff?'

'No—certainly not!' Jassy recoiled in horror. 'I must have about a hundred francs' worth inside my nose already.'

'Now you see why some perfume houses, even good ones, use no real flower essence at all—only man-made chemicals, which smell exactly like the real thing.'

'I didn't know that.' She was astonished. 'I thought——'

'You thought that when a perfume smells of Bulgarian roses or geranium or jasmine, it must be made from those ingredients. Sorry to shatter your romantic illusions, but not necessarily. Michel here could produce a perfect artificial jasmine absolute for a few thousand francs a kilo, but we still prefer to use many of the real essential oils.'

'And that's what makes your perfumes so expensive,' she said, 'so much dearer than Chanel and Yves St Laurent, for instance?'

'Oh, so you've been sussing out the opposition.'

She wasn't altogether sure that she liked his tone, so she said rather tartly, 'Well, after all, I am in the business now. The last couple of days, I've taken a close look at all the perfume displays in the stores in town. I really think we might——' She broke off abruptly.

'Might what?'

'Oh, nothing,' she said hastily. After all, when they were getting on so well, it seemed a pity to risk the thunder clouds of his anger if she had the temerity to start putting the firm—*his* firm—to rights.

'Hmm.' He was still eyeing her consideringly, but then, 'I'd like your opinion on one of our products—as someone who does not wear them from choice.'

Jassy felt herself colour slightly. 'If I'd known I was coming here this morning I would of course have used one of your perfumes.'

'But not otherwise?'

Well, he was asking her. She took a deep breath and dived in, feet first. 'No.' Conscious of Michel at the far end of the room, she kept her voice low. 'Since I began working for Armand I've tried most of them—he used to give me samples. Of course, I always told him I liked them—and no, I wasn't creeping round him,' she added with a little flare of anger as he raised a sardonic eyebrow. 'He was so proud of the firm that he'd built up that I couldn't bear to hurt him—but none of them really appealed to me. I'm sorry,' she spread her hands in slightly embarrassed apology, 'but that's the way it is.'

'Oh, don't apologise. We're always *most* grateful

for feedback from our consumers. You'll have to tell me in detail some time—but not here,' with a glance at Michel, 'where you think we're going wrong.'

Jassy eyed him suspiciously, but could not detect any hint of sarcasm in his tone. He turned away and, taking a key from his pocket, unlocked a drawer and took out a small green glass bottle.

'Try this.'

She caught sight of the label. 'Oh, it's Chantal. But I——'

'Ssh!' He leaned across and very gently put a finger on her lips. 'It is *not* Chantal—it's a new perfume, which as yet has no name. It's labelled Chantal, but that's only to deceive any of our competitors' spies who might come looking. Oh, yes,' he went on grimly, as she gaped at him, 'the oh, so refined business of perfumery can be extremely sordid on occasion. I could tell you some things——' he inclined his head tantalisingly '—but I shall not, until I am sure of your discretion.'

From another drawer he took a bottle of surgical spirit, some of which he dabbed on to a piece of cotton wool.

'Now, where is your perfume?' When she looked at him blankly, he went on impatiently, 'Where exactly did you put your perfume this morning?'

'Behind my ears, I think, but——' Too late, Jassy jerked back.

'Keep still—I must remove it,' he commanded, and she forced herself to stand rigid as she felt his fingers methodically pass the cotton wool to and fro behind first one ear and then the other.

'Now, where else?'

He was standing right in front of her so that, although somewhere at the end of the room Michel was moving about, all she could see was Alain Deville, all she was aware of was him.

'I——' she swallowed an obstruction in her throat '—I only put it there—behind my ears.'

'Tch!' He shook his head reprovingly. 'Surely you know that if a woman is going to the trouble of using perfume, she should apply it to all her pulse points, so that the warmth of her body will make it flower into life.'

He unscrewed the bottle cap and, tilting it slightly, put a little on his finger.

'Behind the ears, yes,' quite beyond movement, she felt him lightly touch one ear, then the other, 'but then the temple,' her eyes half closed under the seductive smell, the hypnotic softness of his voice and the feel of his fingers sensuously brushing across her forehead, 'the throat,' and she knew that he must be aware of the pulse flickering with terrifying irregularity at the base of her neck, 'the wrists,' he caught up first one slim wrist, then the other, 'the crook of the elbow,' she had to break free from this spell, but could only stand obedient under his hands, 'and between the breasts——'

Her eyes flew wide open and one hand clutched protectively at the neckline of her dress.

'No!' she said loudly. 'You mustn't. I——'

He chuckled softly. 'Do not upset yourself, *ma chère*. I was merely going to say that although you should also, of course, always apply perfume between your breasts, Michel might think it a little strange if I were to do so now, so that——' he paused fractionally '—is a pleasure I—*we* shall have to postpone.'

She felt the crimson tide flood into her cheeks, but he had already turned away to replace the perfume in its drawer, and seemed mercifully unaware of the effect of his words.

Raising her wrist, she sniffed tentatively.

'Not too close,' he ordered, though without turning round. Did he have eyes in the back of his head? Probably, she thought, and hastily lifted her nose a few inches.

'You must let the base notes drift up to you first.'

'Mmm. I think I like it,' she said cautiously.

'Yes, I thought you would.' When he caught her expression, he laughed. 'No, I'm not being a smug, complacent male. It's just that women tend to like perfumes from the same fragrance group. You use Mitsouko—you will also, I imagine, like Ma Griffe and Quadrille.'

'Well, yes I do, but how——'

'They all all Chypre-type perfumes, and so is this. So I was fairly safe in assuming that, for once, I had found a Deville perfume of which even the fastidious nose of Mademoiselle Powers would approve.'

Jassy sniffed again and caught his eye over her hand. 'You seem to have studied them very carefully—women, I mean.'

He gave her a long look. 'But always in the line of duty, I assure you.'

'Oh yes, I'm sure.' She returned his look with one of her own, and he laughed.

'Well—perhaps not quite always. But promise me that from now on you will always wear perfume properly. As a *parfumeur* I break my heart,' and he put his hand to where—if he had one—his heart would be, 'to see a woman not use perfume correctly. After all, you surely remember what Coco Chanel said?'

He paused and looked at her, brows raised. What was coming now? He was teasing her again—or rather, not exactly teasing her; it was much more disturbing than that, and she could feel the ground slipping away under her feet.

'No, I don't know,' she snapped, 'but no doubt you're going to tell me.'

'When asked where a woman should wear her perfume, she replied, wherever she wants to be kissed. That conjures up some very pleasant images, *n'est-ce pas*?'

But before she could even begin to think of an answer, he went on, 'And now, I think you should be able to detect the middle notes.'

He lifted her arm and sniffed, not at her wrist but at the crook of her elbow. 'Yes, your body warmth has released the scents. Smell.'

Jassy lowered her head. 'Mmm, it's beautiful. Is it jasmine?'

She glanced up enquiringly and caught his eyes on her face. Just for a moment, it seemed to be his turn to be thrown off balance; he stared at her, then said in a rather husky voice, 'That's right—jasmine, plus bergamot and oak moss. So you approve?'

She took another luxurious sniff. 'Oh, yes, Alain—it's a really wonderful perfume.'

A smile flickered across his features.

'So we have crossed the first hurdle.'

'What do you mean?'

'In your new-found enthusiasm for all things Deville you called me Alain, my dear *Jassy*.'

Neither of them spoke a word on the way back to the villa. Alain's eyes and attention seemed to be concentrated exclusively on the busy road ahead, while Jassy sat in a cloud of perfume, fidgeting with her bag and trying not to feel her skin, still warm from the touch of those tanned fingers that now curved negligently around the steering-wheel.

When he pulled up outside the Villa Chantal she turned to him. 'Thank you—that was very interesting.'

Appalled to hear how stilted she sounded, she hesitated, thought, I am definitely going to regret this, but was still opening her mouth to invite him in, when he said, 'Yes, I think I will have that drink now, thank you,' and gestured her up the steps to the front door.

In the living-room, in a determined effort to regain the initiative, she said pointedly, 'Do please sit down,' just as he was about to drop on to the sofa.

'Thank you, Jassy—I will.'

She turned away to the drinks cupboard and surveyed the contents. 'What can I offer you? Pernod, Martini——'

'A small dry Martini will be fine.'

She poured two, set one down at his elbow, then sat down in the furthest armchair. He took a sip, then remarked conversationally, 'You know, I never appreciated until now what a beautiful room this is.'

'Oh, yes, it faces south, so——'

'Of course, what it has lacked until now is to be set off by a lovely young woman.'

Jassy, just reaching for her drink, jarred her hand against it, sending half of it spilling across the polished table.

'Oh, dear,' said Alain, 'I hope this isn't becoming a habit—you upsetting your drink whenever I'm around.'

'No, it isn't,' she snapped, irritably dabbing at the liquid with a tissue. 'I just wish to goodness you wouldn't *say* things like that!' And yet, beneath the irritation, she was aware of a tiny, *frightening* glow of pleasure. In a desperate attempt to stifle it, she went on, raising her brows in mock enquiry, 'In any case, *Monsieur Deville*, I wasn't born yesterday, you know. Surely every Frenchman falls out of his cradle with a gallant compliment on the tip of his baby tongue.'

He laughed. 'Well, yes, it's a necessary part of our public image, I admit. But when I see a woman in a dress which so perfectly sets off her beauty, I——'

'You swing into action, the soft soap firing on all cylinders,' she said sweetly, but then, jumpy as a cat, she sprang to her feet again and went across to the window.

She stood looking out at the garden, her back to him as she struggled to regain her fragile poise. That sudden, unexpected compliment had thrown her— and, much more than the actual words, the expression which for a few seconds she was sure she had glimpsed in those unrevealing grey eyes. A truce with this man was one thing; she had welcomed the cessation of hostilities, even temporarily, but——

Beside her was a bowl of flowers and she began compulsively rearranging the already perfect arrangement that Céline had created from the bouquet he had brought her. That gorgeous bouquet— just another of his ploys to get under her defences. . .

But she couldn't stand here all afternoon, and Alain obviously had no intention of leaving. Then, gratefully, she remembering something which could get them back on a more formal footing, and swung round to him.

'You said you had a business proposition to put to me?'

'Ah, yes.' He gave her a rather odd little smile. 'But not business, I think. I said merely a proposition, if you remember.'

'Well, OK then, but what is it?'

'Just this—I really think, my dear Jassy, that, all things considered, you should marry me.'

CHAPTER FOUR

'WHAT?' Jassy stared at him, her green eyes enormous with shock. 'You're crazy—or is this some kind of sick joke?' Though Alain Deville did not look the kind of man to play childish tricks.

'No joke, I promise you, Jassy.'

'B-but you can't be serious,' she stammered.

'Oh, I assure you, I am completely serious. I was never more serious about anything in my life.'

'But you don't even like me—let alone *love* me!'

'Does that matter?'

'Yes, of course it matters.'

He laughed unaffectedly. 'So you really are a sweet, old-fashioned romantic at heart, after all.'

'I most certainly am not,' she retorted indignantly, 'but even so——' She broke off, and, struggling to pull her scattered wits together, stood up abruptly. 'Thank you, Monsieur Deville,' cold formality was her best weapon here, 'but I have to refuse your kind proposal. And now, if you'll excuse me,' she glanced pointedly at the ormulu clock, 'it's very late, and——'

'I have not yet finished.'

Instead of obediently hauling himself to his feet, Alain lounged back even more deliberately into the sofa, then patted the cushion beside him. 'I'm tired of shouting our private affairs across the room to you. Come here.'

Jassy tapped her foot, completely nonplussed. Should she have him thrown out on his ear? Very tempting. On the other hand, though, she could hear one of the maids moving around in the hall outside, so any altercation would no doubt be all round the Deville bush-telegraph system by teatime, and she cringed inwardly at the gossip that would provoke.

'Very well, but please don't take long,' she said in her most businesslike voice, and sat down, carefully leaving a cushion's width between them, but then, when he did not immediately speak, she went on tautly, 'Well, I'm waiting.'

'Let me explain just why our marriage would be such an excellent idea, for both of us.'

She laughed abruptly. 'Considering you're planning the rest of my life for me, you sound about as emotional as if you were negotiating a new wage deal for your work-force!'

He gave her a slanting look. 'I'm so sorry—I forgot you are a romantic. Would you prefer me perhaps to go down on one knee?'

His mocking tone set her teeth on edge. 'I would prefer you to leave, right now.'

'My dear Jassy. I really cannot understand your objections——'

'No, well, you wouldn't, would you, being such a——'

'After all, there is a long tradition of marriage alliances between our two countries. When your English kings were not busy burning the French peasants' roofs over their heads, they were pursuing our princesses with equal enthusiasm.'

'Yes, and how many of those arranged matches were happy, do you think?'

'As happy as most marriages, I imagine.'

Shocked, Jassy gave him a swift sideways glance. 'That's a pretty cycnical view.'

He shrugged carelessly. 'I have not reached the ripe old age of thirty-six without gaining my fair share of cynicism.'

'And I suppose you'd think it was quite right and proper for those kings to take a mistress within a week of the marriage?'

Another shrug. 'Why not?' He gave her a faint smile. 'But in your case, *ma chère* Jassy, that would not arise, I assure you.'

'Oh, I'm so glad about that,' she said tartly. 'But as I've no intention of——'

'No one married to you would ever look elsewhere. You possess within you everything a man could possibly desire.'

The openly sexual meaning in his words almost threw her, but somehow she held on to her composure, outwardly at least, determined that he should not have the satisfaction of seeing her increased discomfiture.

'These alliances,' she said with forced casualness, 'they were usually made against a common enemy, weren't they? Just who is the enemy in our case?'

'You've met them,' he said, with more than a hint of grimness.

'Oh, you mean the rest of your family?' He nodded. 'Well, they made their feelings towards me plain enough—come to that, you did as well—but what have they got against *you*?'

'There are—problems with the company,' he said sombrely, and she saw his face tighten into a frown.

'Tell me about them.' Then, as he looked sharply at her, 'Well, after all, whether you like it or not, I am one of you now, aren't I?'

He hesitated. 'Yes—you should know. And before the next board meeting.'

'Oh, yes. This Friday, isn't it?' she said, with a slight sinking feeling. Monsieur Ridoux had phoned her with the details, and it was a session that she certainly wasn't looking forward to.

'Yes, I shall pick you up here at ten.'

Jassy opened her mouth to protest hotly that she was perfectly capable of arranging her own transport, then closed it quickly. Arguments over Friday could wait until Friday.

'Deville Perfumes is not doing as well at the moment as many of its competitors. I have been warning them for over a year now, but Armand has been unable to take an active part in the business for some time and the other four members of the board have refused to budge, thanks to Tante Monique. Given the chance, I could pull the firm round, I know I could. But every time I've tried to make a move, I've been blocked.'

She heard the vibrant anger in his voice and against her will felt some sympathy for his frustration. He was obviously proud of the company—she had glimpsed something of that pride this morning, when he had shown her the factory—and she could imagine how the others just sat around waiting for the rewards of his unremitting hard work to drop like fruit from the bush into their greedy laps.

'But surely things are different now.' She spoke in a softer tone.

Alain gave a harsh laugh. 'Are they? You'll see on Friday that they're busy forcing me into a corner—they want a complete sell-out now that Armand is dead. Rumours have been circulated, no doubt from inside the family, that we're in trouble, and I know that at least two of our rivals, who see us as a lame duck ripe for the plucking, are preparing to launch hostile take-over bids. Monique and my cousins want out, and Louis is a cipher whom I can't be sure of.'

Of course. Light dawned. 'And you want to be sure of me?'

'Yes, I do.'

Well, at least he was doing her the honour of not prevaricating.

'What you mean is that with my shares combined with yours, you could be certain of getting your own way.'

'Precisely.'

She'd known all along that this was just a financial agreement he was proposing, but even so she felt a momentary stab of pain before the hot anger rose inside her.

'So I was right. This marriage proposal of yours is just a cold-blooded business proposition.'

'Business, yes. Cold-blooded? Oh, no, Jassy. With you, never.'

And without warning she felt his hand slide under her curls to softly caress her neck.

Her whole body went rigid, but then, as she tensed to leap to her feet, his hand moved to her shoulder, his fingers digging into the soft flesh and forcing her back down.

'Not just yet, Jassy. *I* decide when this interview ends.'

She wriggled from under the heavy weight of his arm and swung round on him, her eyes blazing.

'D'you want to know something? You make me sick—you really do! How long ago was it—two days?—you were telling me you wouldn't dirty your hands on me. And now, because I won't sell you my shares, you think you can seduce them out of me!'

'Seduce?' His mock-innocent expression only added to her bitterness.

'Maybe I shouldn't blame you, though. After all, how could a cheap little tart like me resist the irresistible Alain Deville?'

'*Taisez-vous*!' A dull red flush spread across his cheeks, so that she saw for the first time the faint puffiness that still remained from her slap. 'I am not offering you seduction, but honourable marriage, remember.'

'But why do you have to marry me, anyway? What makes you think I wouldn't vote against any take-over bid? Oh, not for your sake—although I just might side with you against that gorgon of an aunt of yours—but for Armand's. I'm certain he didn't leave me those shares for me to sell out the firm to the first bidder.'

'But why shouldn't you? You'd make a handsome killing overnight.'

'Oh, so that's what's bugging you.' When he directed a look of cold enquiry at her, Jassy went on, 'Sell and run—that's what you'd expect from a grubby little gold-digger, isn't it? So—why aren't I?'

'That is exactly the question I have been asking myself.'

'And what conclusion have you come to? Do tell me.'

'No firm conclusion, although I admit that I am wondering if you are even more devious than I at first thought.'

'Well, thank you. I suppose it takes one to spot one,' she snapped.

'Devious? Hmm.' He looked at her appraisingly. 'If that is the case, I think we would make a good pair, you and I.'

'A good pair,' she echoed. 'But not equals, of course. I suppose you think that, as your dutiful little wife, I would obey your every command, oh, lord and master.'

'I would hope so, yes,' he said evenly.

'But you see, I just might disappoint you. I might not be quite so ready to jump through every hoop you pointed at me.'

'I'm quite sure that you would not,' his tone was dry, 'at first. But you see, Jassy, I would so much enjoy breaking you in——'

'Oh, I can quite imagine that,' she said in her nastiest voice. 'If ever a man had sadist written all over him——'

'You remind me so much of a young, unschooled mare I had when I was a boy—even down to the colour. Soraya was a chestnut too,' he ran his eyes slowly over her hair, 'and she also was wayward, obstinate, beautiful. But when I had mastered her, riding was a supreme pleasure for both of us—for me to ride without the need of whip or spurs, and for her to be ridden.'

Jassy was frustratingly aware of the hot betraying colour brought to her cheeks at the images his words created, but with a supreme effort she just managed to keep her voice cool.

'I'm sorry to disabuse you, but I really don't think that you're the man to—break me in.'

'We shall see, Jassy, we shall see.' Alain paused. 'You have no lover here in Biarritz, I know, but,' as she went to burst in angrily, 'have you a lover in England?'

'That's no concern of yours!'

'Oh, but it is. Have you?'

'All right, damn you. I haven't.'

'I find that difficult to believe.'

'No, no, no, I have not got a lover in England— or anywhere. Satisfied?' She almost spat it at him.

Enough was enough, or in his case more than enough. But even as she braced herself to jump to her feet, his arm, which had been draped negligently along the top of the sofa, descended with the speed of a striking snake and, fastening on her arm, dragged her bodily across the expanse of sofa to him.

'Let me go! You're hurting me——'

But he brought her up hard against him, and for a few seconds they stared into each other's angry faces. Then, as she read the intention in his steel-grey eyes, she tried to draw back.

'No——'

But her protest was blotted out, as he forced her

head back and his mouth came down to claim hers in a savage kiss. One of his hands slid up to grip her curls, so tightly that the pain brought stinging tears to her eyes; the other went to the small of her back, straining her to him so that she was trapped. Her physio training had given her a muscular power which was belied by her slim frame, but even so she fought despairingly, knowing that she was hopelessly outmatched, while her opponent was as careless of those struggles as though she lay quite unresisting in his embrace.

She tried to close her lips against him, but he forced them apart, his tongue thrusting into her bruised mouth to ravage it cruelly. She was almost suffocating, the only sound she could make angry, gasping little grunts which he contemptuously ignored. Her senses were reeling, until she thought she would pass out, but then she clawed despairingly at one last coherent thought.

She made herself stop struggling, willing herself to go limp under his hands, then deliberately let her mouth go slack and gave a little moan. At her apparent surrender, Alain loosened his grip just sufficiently for her to move her mouth from his. She slid it gently along his jaw, as though in a tender caress, then, as she came to the soft flesh just over the jaw bone, she sank in her teeth as hard as she could.

The effect was instantaneous.

'You little bitch!'

He drew back sharply, jerking away with a furious oath, and she broke free at last, scrambling to her feet. As she gulped in the oxygen, the room lurched around her, but then she put her hand to her bruised mouth and glowered down at him.

'W-what an arrogant swine you are!' She was still sobbing for breath. 'You really can't believe, c-can you, that I should actually turn you down? Just because every other woman, no doubt, comes running at the flick of your little finger, you thought that one kiss would have me grovelling at your feet!'

He had got out a handkerchief and was holding it to his jaw. With a spasm of anguished guilt, she saw blood staining the white linen, and when he lifted it she could see the bluish line of angry teeth marks. Oh God, what had he reduced her to?

'I was wrong about one thing, anyway.' His voice was level, but she sensed with a flicker of trepidation that he was only holding himself in control with a tremendous effort. No doubt women didn't usually bite Alain Deville and escape to tell the tale. 'You're nothing better than a spitting, snarling, vicious little wildcat.'

An apology had been trembling on her lips, but she wouldn't waste her sympathy.

'Oh, you've forgotten all the rest!' she hurled at him. 'Let me tell you, once and for all, scheming little gold-diggers like me have certain standards to keep up. I have no intention of marrying anyone, and from what I've seen of you, absolutely none of marrying you, even—no, *especially* to safeguard your precious firm!'

Alain stared up at her, his lips a thin line, but then, biting back whatever retort he had been about to make, he stood up. Jassy's whole body tensed—she was terrified that he was about to seize hold of her again—but, without even glancing in her direction, he strode across to the door. He opened it, then said, still without looking at her, 'I shall pick you up on Friday at ten, as we arranged.'

'Very well.'

Unable to trust herself to utter another word, she stood motionless as he went out. She heard his footsteps in the hall, the front door closing and, a few moments later, the car engine roar into life.

Her legs were trembling under her and she sank on to the nearest chair. Then, as she put up her shaking hands, she realised that tears were cascading down her face.

'I'm sorry, but I cannot agree with you there, Robert. If you look at the figures. . .'

Alain's cool voice flowed smoothly on, keeping an iron grip on his fellow board members. Jassy studied him dispassionately. The way he was chairing the meeting reminded her of nothing so much as an animal trainer, cracking the invisible whip at his snarling charges. She herself had been more than content to stay inconspicuously at the far end of the table, watching the fascinating interplay of views and personalities.

Certainly, the picture that was emerging of the company's state was just as parlous as he had indicated. Her eyes strayed to Sophie Larbaud, who, Jassy gathered, was based in Paris as head of the firm's European Sales division, and who was sitting alongside him. Mid-thirties, she guessed, attractive, beautifully groomed—did his taste run to violet-eyed blondes? she wondered. The lead of her pencil,

with which she had been creating a line of swirling
doodles down the margin of her pad, snapped suddenly with the sound of a tiny rifle shot and, catching
his eye down the table, she hastily reached forward
to take up another pencil. . .

The extremely gloomy set of figures for the past
six months' sales which Mademoiselle Larbaud had
presented had been Monique's cue to launch into
her obviously pre-planned spiel in favour of selling
out, before the situation became even worse. Robert
and Martine, loyal cohorts of their formidable
mother, had then chipped in with equally clearly
prearranged contributions and, as Alain had pre-
dicted, Louis, although doing very little except puff
on a fat, noxious cigar, seemed to be drifting along
with them.

Alain had said nothing to Jassy about his strategy
on the drive to the meeting—in fact, they had hardly
exchanged a single word since he had collected her.
She had been waiting for him, having spent the
previous quarter of an hour prowling restlessly up
and down the hall, and when she heard the imperious car horn she went down the steps, all too
conscious of the scrutiny of a pair of cool grey eyes,
taking in every detail of her white cotton sailcloth
suit, with its longish square-cut jacket and short
skirt, and the fine black cotton blouse, which after
agonised indecision she had picked on as being the
most suitable outfit in her wardrobe for this particular occasion. But he had said nothing as she climbed
in beside him, acknowledging her with the merest
grunt.

As he leaned past her to close her door, taking

very obvious care not to touch any part of her
anatomy, she saw with horror that, adorning that
hard jaw, was a large square of pink sticking plaster.
Although he was already pulling away and did not
look at her, he must have sensed her eyes on him,
for he said evenly, 'For anyone who asks, I cut
myself very badly shaving yesterday, though I realise
that, of course, people don't normally cut themselves with an electric shaver.'

Jassy looked at him, conscience-stricken. There
was even still, just perceptible, the shadowy outline
on his cheek where her hand had struck him that
stinging blow.

'I-I'm sorry,' she whispered miserably.

Alain raised his eyebrows. 'For what? Maiming
me for life, or merely for making my existence even
more trying than it is already?' So she had turned
her head away to watch the geranium-pink roofs and
pretty white villas of Biarritz slide past the window.

She had half expected that he would spend the
short journey to Bayonne trying to ensure that,
despite their personal animosity, she would not act
out of malice—or at least attempting to discover
which way she intended to jump with her thirty per
cent of the shares.

The previous night she had even had a very
pleasurable dream, in which he was on his knees to
her, begging her not to scupper him and the firm,
but in the cold light of morning such grovelling from
this proud, inflexible man had seemed an unlikely
fantasy, to say the least. Even so, she was not sure
whether she was relieved or disappointed when they
arrived and he had not spoken another word.

They had entered the boardroom together but, seeing the others already gathered like vultures in what looked very like a conspiratorial knot at the far end of the room, Jassy had peeled away hastily and taken up her seat as far as possible from him.

She now realised that he must have decided that the best strategy was reasoned attack, courteously letting each of them have their say before coming back with calmly expressed arguments countering each point in turn. Several times, though, Monique had succeeded in interrupting him, with increasing shrillness, and Jassy had all but heard the clash of steel from their invisible swords. How long would he let this go on for, she wondered, before he called for a vote?

'You have not yet contributed to our discussion, Mademoiselle Powers.' Her pencil skidded across the pad as Alain, for the first time, spoke directly at her. 'As someone who informs me that she is not over-impressed with our present range of products, perhaps you could favour us with your views.'

So he was really putting her on the spot, and yet, as she looked full at him, she sensed, if no one else did, that beneath the smooth exterior there was an inner tension, even uncertainty. Yes, she realised, almost with elation, he really was unsure of how she intended to act.

'Thank you, Monsieur Deville.' She sounded coolly composed, though under cover of the table her hands were twisting endlessly in her lap. 'You and the other members of the board are so much more experienced in these matters than I am, but since you ask me, I think,' she almost felt the air in the room stop breathing, 'I think there is only one response we can make to these take-over bids. We must fight them.'

'Tch!' With an exclamation of disgust, Monique slapped both hands on the table. But Alain, too skilled a poker player to show open relief, only allowed himself the merest flicker of a smile.

'You have some reasons for your opinion—other than pure sentiment, of course?' Martine enquired sweetly.

'Well, yes, I have, as a matter of fact.' Jassy was not going to allow herself to be riled by this over-indulged young woman. 'As I understand it, at least two of our competitors are very interested in taking us over. If, even with our current sales figures, we——'

'We?' Martine interrupted. 'It is amazing, *mademoiselle*, how easily you slip into the *we*. No doubt it follows months of preparation.'

'—if we can attract such interest, surely we have much greater potential than some of us seem to appreciate.'

She turned to Alain, who was leaning back in his chair, watching her across the bridge of his fingers. 'You're quite right, Monsieur Deville. I am not very impressed with our current range and I think it could be improved, both in perfumes and cosmetics, but that's really just my personal taste. No, much more than that, it's our image that needs to be changed.'

Catching up her white leather bag, she pulled out a notebook and a sheaf of papers. 'As well as going round all the local stores, taking a good look at their displays, I've bought up some back numbers of *Elle* and *Marie Claire* and taken out all the perfumery ads, to compare ours to our main competitors'.'

She riffled through the papers and, pulling out several, laid them in front of her. 'For example, there's this one.' She jabbed a finger. 'It seems to be our latest—both magazines carried it last month. Look at it!' She held it up in a dramatic gesture. 'Does this really grab you? I mean,' she corrected herself hastily, 'would it make you want to rush out and buy an enormous bottle of Milady? It's so drab, so Thirtyish——'

'But, Mademoiselle Powers,' Monique cut in, 'perhaps it has escaped your notice that Thirties nostalgia is very much *à la mode*.'

Jassy nodded. 'Yes, you're quite right. But if you look at *these* ads,' she swiftly held up half a dozen, 'and compare them with ours, I think you'll agree that there is a subtle difference. Ours are just drab "Thirties" Thirties, these others have a modern, chic sparkle to them that women want today.'

'And you, of course, are an expert on what women want.' There was an unpleasant undertone in Monique's voice, but Jassy chose to ignore it.

'Well, I am a woman,' she pointed out reasonably, then went on. 'And there's another way in which I think we're projecting an old-fashioned image. Our ads are about as sexy as fish fingers. Look at these for Chantal.' She held up several, one after the other. 'Chantal is quite a heavy, seductive type— one of the Oriental family of perfumes, I believe,' she flashed Alain a swift glance—that should show him she'd been doing her homework, 'and yet all these ads, with slight variations, just have a bottle of the perfume and in the background a woman, either at her dressing-table or her wardrobe, but in every case fully dressed, even down to her coat in this one——'

'What's wrong with that?' Robert broke in aggressively. 'It's a sable coat, isn't it?'

'And you're comparing ours with something like this, I suppose.' Martine's long fingers reached across for another of the torn-out pages. 'A bed. . .hectares of naked flesh. Do we really need to sink to the level of a cheap porno film?'

'For heaven's sake!' Jassy was indignant. 'There's nothing pornographic about this ad.' She studied it. 'It's beautiful—like a Botticelli painting, all those delicate lines and shades. But in any case, can I remind you that this company's sales are way ahead of ours?'

'Well,' Monique again, 'if boosting our sales depends on this kind of vulgarity——'

'It is not vulgar. And in any case, Madame Deville,' Jassy could feel herself being swept along by the tide of battle, 'surely perfumes are meant to be applied to a woman's body, not her clothes. And for that matter, exactly the same applies to the publicity for our men's range.'

She swung round on Alain, who was still leaning back in his chair, and caught a gleam in his grey eyes. He was clearly getting secret amusement from this little confrontation, and particularly from her performance, she strongly suspected. In a flash of sudden devilment, she demanded, 'You wouldn't waste a body perfume on your clothes, would you, *monsieur*?'

Just for a moment he looked almost disconcerted by her unexpected attack, then, 'Indeed not, *mademoiselle*—and I would certainly never just dab it behind my ears.'

He was looking directly at her and, in spite of herself, she laughed out loud.

'Oh, so that's the way of it.' Monique's sharp black eyes flickered from one to the other, then she began gathering together her papers. 'There is no point in prolonging this discussion. It is perfectly clear which way Mademoiselle Powers intends to vote—and why. First my unfortunate brother-in-law, and now my nephew——'

'What?' Jassy felt herself turn scarlet with temper. 'Let me put you right on one thing, Madame Deville. Your precious nephew—just two days ago, I refused——'

'Right,' Alain's voice cut in smooth as silk, 'I take it that, for the moment at least, we resist strongly all hostile bids, and if there is no further business, the meeting is closed.'

Jassy expelled her breath, then, still simmering, gathered up all the papers and stuffed them into her bag. The others had gone, leaving only Alain and Sophie Larbaud in close conversation over by the window. She hesitated, then got up and began to walk towards the door.

'Mademoiselle Powers, can I have a word with you, please?' His cool voice stopped her in her tracks.

'Oh, and that other thing, Alain.' Sophie was speaking. 'Can we talk about it over the weekend?'

'I'm sorry, Sophie, but I'll be tied up all week-end—it will have to wait until Monday.'

She put her face up for him to kiss her on both cheeks, but then, turning away, she shot a swift glance from him to Jassy and back again. The silent appraisal, though totally different from Monique's gimlet-eyed look, was, for Jassy, somehow just as disturbing. She smiled at the other woman, though, and they shook hands, then she waited as Alain came towards her.

'I can easily get a taxi, if you're busy,' she began.

'Certainly not. I want to talk to you.'

'Oh.' Her heart sank. After the morning she'd just had, she was feeling like a wrung-out dish rag. 'Well, all right.' She half pulled out the chair she had just replaced.

'Not here. Over lunch. Oh, don't look so alarmed.' A smile flickered across his austere features. 'No more—propositions, and this time we'll meet on neutral ground, I think. I have reserved a table for us in,' he shot back his white cuff to glance at the slim gold wrist watch, 'half an hour. So, *allons, ma chère.*'

CHAPTER FIVE

'To us.' Alain raised his glass of Pernod.

'To—Parfums Deville,' Jassy replied cautiously, and took a sip of her dry sherry, then, as she set down her glass, she looked around the restaurant with undisguised interest.

It was the first time she had been in the Café de Paris, just about the most exclusive restaurant in Biarritz. The potted palms and airy décor combined with the pretty white lampshades to give it an almost out-of-doors look, while the tables, with their white lace squares laid over pale green linen cloths and set with their gleaming silver and crystal, exuded an air of unostentatious opulence.

She sat back in her chair, smoothing down her skirt and breathing a private sigh of relief. Thank goodness that, driven by her desire not to be put at a disadvantage by the other women, she had dressed up for the board meeting. Really, though, Alain might have given her some warning that he was bringing her on here.

He, of course, was immaculately dressed—although she had the distinct feeling that, whatever the occasion, his clothes would be eminently appropriate. Her eyes skimmed over his light charcoal-grey suit, crisp white poplin shirt, impeccably knotted grey tie. How handsome he was—the hard lines of his tanned face, the thin mouth which, at

least when she was around, could close like a rat
trap but was now softer, more relaxed. . . And what
charming company he was, when he wasn't hurling
abuse at her or trying to wheedle his way under her
guard. . .

Through his black lashes, she could just catch the
glint of his grey eyes as, head slightly bent, he circled
his glass round and round the exact same spot on the
cloth. That faint flush on his cheekbones—surely it
wasn't the remnants of her slap? No—it was a flush
of triumph. He'd won the battle this morning—but
only with her help.

She felt a pricking of unease. Had she, by her
words, committed herself irrevocably to his side?
She really ought to assert her independence—and
right away, before he got any wrong ideas.

'You were very sure of yourself, weren't you?' she
said.

He raised his eyes to meet hers.

'In what way?'

'Well, you told me you'd reserved this table. That
must have been before the meeting, so——' she
lifted her slim shoulders '——you were very sure of
yourself—or of me.'

'Oh, no, Jassy.' He gave her a faint smile. 'I would
never allow myself to be sure of you. I think that
would be very unwise. However, I did hope—
entirely for Armand's sake, not mine, of course,' he
lightly mocked her, 'that on this occasion, at least,
you would see fit to act in accord with my wishes.'

She waited while the waiter set in front of her
wafer-thin slices of marinated salmon and, for Alain,
a fish terrine, prettily decorated with pistachio nuts,

but then, as soon as he was out of earshot, 'Yes, it's true. For Armand's sake, I did support you, but I must warn you that you can't always depend on that. I could never back you in anything which I didn't think was for the good of the company.'

'In that case, Jassy,' she watched as he neatly dissected a piece of terrine, 'I shall have to make sure, shan't I, that absolutely everything I do meets with your whole-hearted approval?' And while she was still working out what might possibly lie behind that innocuous statement, he pointed the tip of his knife at her plate. 'Now eat, and *bon appétit*.'

'Mmm, that was marvellous!'

Jassy laid down her knife and fork and sat back, dabbing at her lips with her napkin. A light-as-air round of flaky pastry, filled with lobster and *foie gras*, followed by a tournedos, with *pommes surprises* and a purée of spinach—no wonder the waistband of her skirt seemed to have shrunk a size! Surreptitiously, she opened the top button, then, catching Alain's grin across the table, she pulled a rueful face.

'I shall have to live on salad for the next week!'

'And do you need to diet—surely not?'

His eyes skimmed over her figure and she said quickly, 'Well, not usually. My work's been so physical that I burned off all the extra calories— and, of course, I haven't been able to indulge in many meals like this, until now——'

She broke off in confusion, cursing her rash tongue for leading her into territory she wanted to forget, today at least, but Alain looked at her very straight, his eyes sombre.

'Until your—good fortune? Yes, well, enough—perhaps more than enough—has been said on that matter, I think. What do you say we declare a truce—an armed truce, of course,' a faint smile, 'but a truce none the less?'

He'd thrown some horrible, wounding insults at her, but—she smiled unhesitatingly and held out her hand.

'Of course.'

But instead of shaking it, he took it and, bending his head, brushed sensuously across the palm with his lips, so that little prickles like pins and needles ran up her arm. When he at last released her, she stared blindly at him for an instant, then jerked her hand back, clutching it with the other one under cover of the tablecloth.

'And the company really is safe now?' The words came out louder than she had intended, so that the couple at the next table glanced across at her curiously.

'From hostile bidders, you mean? Yes—so long as your thirty per cent stays where it is, snugly tucked up alongside mine.' She didn't altogether like the image, but she let it go. 'It is just fortunate that Armand resisted the temptation to go public years ago. If we had institutional shareholders to worry about as well as the family, we could be in real trouble.'

'So we're all right, then?'

'Well, for the moment, but we still have those

falling sales figures to contend with. And that is where you can help.'

'Me? Oh, I don't think——' Jassy began dubiously.

'Now, come! Is this the fearless Jassy Powers who slew the awesome Tante Monique this morning?'

He was teasing her, she knew, and she gave him a rueful smile.

'I may have covered up fairly plausibly at the meeting, but you know very well, if the others don't, that I'm totally ignorant about perfumes and the rest of our business. Really, I know no more than the average woman in the street.'

He shook his head at her. 'No, Jassy, I'm quite sure that you will never be average. In the street— or anywhere else.'

'Stop it!'

'Stop what?' He gave her an innocently enquiring look.

'You know very well what. Seducing me with your eyes.' Oh God, was it really she who'd said that? Hastily she pushed away her half-full wine glass.

'And how would you prefer me to——?'

'As I said,' she broke in desperately, and the couple turned to stare at them again, 'I don't know anything about perfume manufacture.'

Alain hesitated, his eyes glinting, but then, obviously relenting, said, 'But you are intelligent, sensible. I trust your judgement—in some matters, at least. I want to conduct a one-woman opinion poll with you. So,' he was deeply serious now, 'you think our range needs a complete overhaul. What specific ideas do you have?'

* * *

By the time the waiter returned with their lemon sorbets, Jassy's brain was reeling. The combination of the food, the wine—which she was quite unused to at lunchtime—and Alain's rigorous cross-examination was taking its toll.

'And *mademoiselle* would care for some cheese to follow?'

'Oh no, nothing more for me, thank you. I couldn't eat another morsel.'

'Just a little,' Alain urged her, 'to help finish this burgundy.'

The selection on the cheese board was enormous, and she looked across at him appealingly.

'Can you help me choose, please?'

'A little Brie, perhaps—oh, and you must try some of this Laroque Pyrenéean. It is fairly new to me but quite delicious.'

As the waiter cut a piece for her he leaned forward discreetly. 'Mademoiselle might care to know that Monsieur Laroque himself is lunching with us today.'

He nodded unobtrusively to the far side of the room where a family were just leaving. The man, tall, broad-shouldered, was lifting a toddler in a white smocked dress out of a high-chair. A slightly older boy, very dark like his father, was waiting gravely alongside a woman, russet-haired, slender build, though Jassy glimpsed beneath the simple lines of her yellow linen shift the slight thickening of early pregnancy.

'Madame Laroque, like mademoiselle,' the waiter's confidential murmur again, 'is from England.'

Jassy looked with even greater interest as the

family made their way outside to the car park, and she continued watching as the man strapped the children into safety seats, then came round to the other side of the car to unlock the door for his wife. As he opened it, just for a moment he rested his hand in a tiny, intimate gesture in the small of her back and she looked up at him. Not a word was spoken, but Jassy, even at that distance, felt flash between the two a shared, perfect happiness.

Quite suddenly, without warning, her insides twisted in a spasm of bleak sadness. For some time now she had felt that, consciously or unconsciously, she had been pursuing her career with such single-mindedness that she had turned her back on marriage. It was only two days ago that she had brusquely rejected Alain's proposal, and with it perhaps the chance of such happiness. But, of course, there was a crucial difference: she and Alain did not love each other, while those two—she watched as the car pulled away out of sight—they were quite obviously going home to a house filled with love. . .

She turned back and realised that Alain was watching her, an enigmatic look in his eyes, and, terrified that he might read even a fraction of her thoughts, she hastily gave all her attention to spreading a water biscuit very neatly with butter.

'Brandy, or a liqueur?'

'Oh, no—thank you.' She smiled across at him. 'I think I've had more than enough to drink already.'

'In that case,' he gave the remnants of his wine a final swirl around the glass and tossed it down his throat, 'if you're quite ready, we really should be going. I have a meeting fixed for this afternoon.'

'Yes, of course.' As he caught the waiter's watchful eye, she smiled again. 'It really was a marvellous meal. Thank you, Alain.'

She shrugged herself into her jacket, which the waiter held for her, then, while Alain settled the bill, wandered outside. Instead of making for the car, though, she walked across the Place Bellevue to the stone latticework balustrade and stood gazing out across the huge hydrangeas to the long line of golden sand of the Grande Plage, stretching in a graceful curve past the brightly striped beach tents, the villas and hotels to the cliffs and lighthouse beyond. This view, for Jassy, had always encapsulated Biarritz—its colour, its vibrancy—and yet today she found herself staring at it almost unseeing.

Alain. . .What a difficult, highly-charged relationship the two of them had, and yet, bit by bit, after that appalling beginning, they did seem to be groping their way towards a better, friendlier even, understanding, a—what had he called it?—an armed truce. And that was just as well, if they were, as co-shareholders, to continue seeing so much of each other. . . On the other hand, though, it would be most unwise, not to say catastrophic, to let that working relationship develop into another kind, the kind where——

She closed her eyes abruptly against a wave of dizziness which swept through her and had to grip hard on the stone railing until that peculiar sensation ebbed as suddenly as it had come. But the images that she had conjured up in those seconds—of her, of Alain. . . Too much alcohol in the middle of the day, plus an overheated imagination, she told herself scornfully. You'd better watch it, Jassy my girl, or——

'And what do you find of such riveting interest?' Alain's voice made her start violently.

'Oh, I——' Still unnerved by those mind pictures, she could not look at him, but then she improvised quickly. 'Those surfers out there.' She pointed to where half a dozen figures were skimming in towards the beach. 'They look so graceful.'

'Yes, but see those two?' She followed his pointing finger. 'They have left it too late to turn.'

As she watched, she saw a crested wave swing in, burying the two surfers in its depths until they struggled clear.

'You knew that was going to happen.' She turned to him now. 'Can you surf?'

He seemed to hesitate, then, 'Yes—at least, I used to.'

'Oh, I'd love to be able to. It must be the next best thing to flying.'

He smiled. 'Maybe—although I do not approve of women surfing here. The waves are too strong for them.'

'Well, of all the chauvinist rubbish!' Jassy flared up instantly. 'Women do surf here—I've seen them. I bet I could learn, if I had a good enough teacher.'

To her horror, she realised that she was now looking directly up at him with what was surely an expression of winsome appeal in her eyes. What on earth was that wine doing to her?

'No, no, Jassy.' He frowned down at her. '*Absolument, non.*'

But she'd gone this far, and all at once it seemed

vitally important to her that she should win this little tussle of wills. She put on a deliberate pout.

'I don't see why.'

'Well, for one thing,' he shot her a wry smile, 'I don't think that I would make a good teacher—I have very little patience.' Tell me something I don't know, she thought. 'And, just when we're getting along so much better,' she heard the teasing note in his voice again, but made herself go on studying a pile of tiny stones that she was scuffing around with the toe of her shoe, 'it seems a pity to put our new understanding so seriously at risk.'

She managed to give a little shrug. 'I'm prepared to take a chance on that, if you are. Look, they're coming in again.' They both turned to watch the dark figures, silhouetted against the brilliant blue of the sea, then she said softly, 'Please, Alain.'

'Oh God—women!' He scowled in exasperation. 'Can you swim well?'

'Oh, yes.' She smiled radiantly at him. 'I got my life-saving badge at school, and——'

'Well, that's a relief. In that case you'll be able to rescue me if I get into difficulties out there.' His grin faded and he seemed to study her intently. 'Does it really mean so much to you?'

No, but you doing something—anything—for me does, she desperately wanted to say, but instead she came out with, 'Of course not—but I do think you owe me a favour.'

'A favour?' He regarded her warily.

'Yes, you know—for voting with you this morning.'

'You little minx!'

He laughed out loud and while she was still smiling back at him, quite unexpectedly, he put his arms around her and kissed her. Unlike that terrible previous time, it was a gentle, undemanding kiss, his lips warm and strangely comforting against hers. And yet when they drew apart they held each other at arm's length for long seconds, staring into one another's eyes, before at last Jassy's gaze flickered and fell before what she read in his.

Alain too seemed all at once anxious to break the tension, which, without warning, had once again spiralled between them and, very deliberately, he looked down at his watch.

'I must go—I am late already.' He frowned, tapping his foot. 'If you really want a lesson, I can give you one tomorrow. I'm busy all day, but shall we say six o'clock tomorrow evening?'

'That would be fine, thank you.' Taking her cue from him, she too became very formal again. 'If that suits you, of course.'

But he ignored her tentative remark.

'I'll find a wet suit for you.'

'Oh, this first time, I don't think——'

'If you surf with me, you wear a wet suit,' he cut in. 'I think we'll go to the Côte des Basques beach. It should be quieter there. I'll pick you up at five-thirty.'

'Oh, no, you needn't bother,' she said hastily. 'I can spend the afternoon there. It's my favourite beach, and——'

But he had already turned away, so she followed him across to the car.

* * *

Jassy, perched on the low stone parapet, her knees
to her chin, was gazing down at the beach. It had
been very crowded all afternoon, with tourists of all
nationalities combined with French weekenders, but
now most people were packing up and leaving to
prepare for the ritual of Saturday evening dinner.
She let her eyes drift with the line of nose-to-tail
departing cars, then saw, with a quick catch of her
throat, a sleek grey Citroën turn the corner and
weave its way down the narrow road.

There was a parking space slightly further along,
and as Alain pulled into it she scrambled off the
wall. Smoothing down her loose turquoise top, she
brushed imaginary sand off her white shorts with a
hand that was not altogether steady, then, picking
up her yellow canvas beach bag and straw hat, she
walked across to him.

Casually dressed in a navy T-shirt and blue denim
shorts, which revealed disturbingly long tanned legs
and muscular thighs, he leaned against the side of
the car, watching her as she came towards him. The
sun was in her eyes so that she felt rather than saw
the intensity of his gaze, but he only said, 'Sorry I'm
a little late. The meeting went on longer than I had
anticipated.'

His brusque greeting was more than matched by
his cool expression, and instinctively Jassy put up
her hand to brush back her damp, unruly curls in a
defensive gesture. Several times that afternoon,
watching the huge Atlantic breakers sweeping in,
she had regretted the impulsive folly two or three
glasses of wine had engendered, and now, seeing

him in this obviously foul mood, she regretted it even more.

'Look, if you'd rather not,' she began, 'I don't mind if——'

'I'm here now,' he said ungraciously, 'so let's get on with it, shall we?'

He opened the car boot and fetched out two wet suits, one of which—a black and purple one—he held out to her.

'This one should fit you. It was mine when I was a teenager.'

He half turned away and, with the supreme unself-consciousness of all Frenchmen, pulled off his T-shirt to reveal his powerful shoulders and sleek, bronzed chest, with its light sprinkling of dark hairs, then unzipped his shorts and stepped out of them. Underneath, he was wearing only the slightest of black briefs, which hugged the taut line of his hips in a kind of intimate caress. There was no paler band of flesh above them—he must sunbathe nude.

Jassy, barely aware of what she was doing, clutched the wet suit to her and stared at him, the blood in her veins suddenly flowing thick and slow, until it almost seemed to congeal. And then, as though alerted by her utter stillness, Alain glanced sharply up at her. For a moment, their eyes locked and held before she turned away in confusion to quickly strip off to her aquamarine cotton bikini and begin struggling with the intractable folds of hot, damp rubber.

'Here—let me help.'

Alain, his body now safely encased in an all-black wet suit, took a firm grip of hers, gave it a sharp jerk, and instantly two armholes revealed themselves. She thrust her hands through, mumbling a 'Thank you', then forced herself to stand quiescent as he pulled up the long crutch-to-chin zip.

'Phew!' She wriggled her shoulders against the hard rubber neckline. 'Now I know how a caterpillar feels when he's about to split his skin!'

He stepped back and studied her critically. 'Actually, it's a good fit—though I must say it never looked quite so ravishing when I was wearing it.'

Well, at least, she thought, a little surge of thankfulness mingling with her twinge of alarm, he did seem to be shaking himself free of his morose mood. She watched as he lifted out two surfboards from the car boot, laid them down on the wall, then rubbed them carefully all over with a block of wax.

As she leaned against the wall beside him, a group of pretty young teenagers, in various stages of undress, sauntered past, and Jassy saw them give Alain a long, lingering once-over. She thought he had been quite unaware of them, but as they piled into an open-top car a few yards further along, he lifted his head and winked complacently at her.

'Well, I'm glad to see you're *so* modest!'

'Certainly I am.' He tossed the wax into the boot, then locked it. 'It gives my wilting thirty-six-year-old male ego a tremendous boost, I can assure you, to be on the receiving end of come-to-bed looks from such nubile young bimbos.'

At that instant, a buggy piled with half a dozen young men roared past, its occupants leaning out, whistling and hurling highly improper suggestions at Jassy. She flushed rose-pink, but their high spirits were irresistible and she laughed out loud, then, turning, saw Alain scowling at her.

'I'm sorry,' she slanted him a demure look from under her lashes, 'but my wilting twenty-seven-year-old female ego needs a boost now and then.'

His scowl deepened for a moment, but then he grinned. '*Touché, ma chère*! Right, let's go.'

Handing her the smaller of the two boards, he led the way to a flight of stone steps which fanned down to the beach. At the bottom, he bent down to fasten the end of her strap around her ankle, then checked that the other end was firmly attached to the board. As she stood looking down at him, suddenly to her horror, she was filled with an almost overwhelming urge to rest her fingers on that dark head, but mercifully, before her hand could move, he straightened up.

At the water's edge he pulled the tight-fitting hood over his head and she followed suit, jamming her unruly curls out of sight. In his black, skin-clinging suit, Alain all at once looked sinister, like a sleek black shark, but then the illusion vanished as, perhaps sensing her uncertainty, he smiled reassuringly at her and they waded out into the shallow water, jumping each broken ripple as it struck them. As the waves grew larger, though, they buffeted her and she could not so easily keep her footing against them.

'Hold on to your board and dive through them,' Alain told her, and obediently, as each wave reared up, she clambered on to her board and lay flat, plunging into the glassy green depths to emerge on the other side, gasping for breath and half blinded by salt water.

'All right?'

Alain, close by her side, yelled against the boom of the waves breaking on the beach and she nodded, grinning happily. Out here, the waves really did seem enormous, but all her fear had miraculously gone, pounded out of her mind by the roar of the water, until she felt only exhilaration.

'Right, this is far enough. Ready to go?'

'Ready.'

He slipped off his own board and, holding on to it with one arm, caught hers, swinging it sharply round to point towards the shore. Treading water to keep himself upright, he held on to her board, gauging the approaching waves. His head was very near hers, but he seemed quite unconscious of her—there was a frown of absolute concentration on his face, his large, suntanned hand white-knuckled as he tensed his grip.

'No. . . No. . . Now——' he yelled as Jassy hesitated for a split second '—get your feet up!'

But the wave had struck them, sweeping her away from him in an avalanche of snow-white water. Clinging desperately to the board, she scrabbled frantically to haul up her feet, but then her precarious balance went and she was tumbled over and over, surfacing after what seemed like half a lifetime and coughing out the sea water which had filled her lungs.

Alain, the water streaming off him, appeared alongside her and caught hold of her arm.

'OK?'

'Yes—fine,' she gasped, and somehow managed to raise a confident smile.

But just then another wave broke against them and she clutched at him, before hastily transferring her grip to her board.

'You have to get the timing just right. Next time I say go—just *go*.'

'Aye, aye, sir.' She half lifted one arm in salute, then quickly replaced it.

'Get your legs up faster. Don't wait till the wave's already on you. Now, get ready.'

Jassy's hands were wet, the board was slippery, her rubber suit was dragging against it, and she struggled ineffectually to clamber up, but instead hung helplessly, half on and half off. Next moment, she felt Alain's hand against her bottom, the fingers outspread, then, with a long, powerful heave, he lifted her up on to it.

'Hold on. . . Wait. . . *Now*!'

And again, as the wave peaked behind them, he thrust her forward with it, and again, after a frenzied struggle, she was snatched up and engulfed by the torrent of water. When she surfaced, Alain, ever watchful, was bobbing beside her. He was spluttering—of course, waiting for her, he too was being caught by every wave.

'I'm sorry,' she gasped. 'I'm awful at it.'

Heaving for breath, she had to speak right in his face for him to catch the words, but he shook his head emphatically.

'Nonsense. Took me years to learn.'

Jassy was quite certain that he was only being kind. She had already seen enough to realise that he was a web-footer—a man as much at ease in the sea as on dry land—but she gave him a grateful smile as he held on to her board while several small waves bobbed along under them.

'You almost got one leg up,' he added encouragingly. 'Next time, jerk yourself forward and bring your legs up sharp behind you. Now, get ready. . .'

They'd been out here for days, surely—the surf pounding deafeningly in their ears, their eyes red and smarting with salt water. Then, at last, when only her stubborn will was keeping her there, another huge wave reared to a crest behind them, Alain gave her a push and she thought, This time I will do it.

As the wave lifted the board, somehow she scrabbled both feet on to it, dragged herself up into a crouch, hung on the narrow sliver of plastic for a few glorious, fleeting—precarious—seconds, then, even as she heard Alain's hoarse yell of triumph, fell clean off into the heart of the wave.

'Great! You made it!'

As she struggled to the surface, he seized the board, which was floating beside her, for her to get a grip on it.

'Right, that's enough for your first time.'

'Oh, no!' she wailed. Her throat and lungs were harsh with salt, muscles she hadn't known she possessed were aching, she could feel the huge bruises on her thigh where the fin of her board had several times caught her, but still she wanted to stay out here forever.

'*Please*, Alain!'

But he shook his head. 'No. The waves are getting higher, and you're very tired.'

Firmly, he turned her board round towards the shore, but she put her hand on his wrist.

'Look, you haven't surfed at all. I'll go in, I promise, but——' as he hesitated '—you can make the rest of my lesson an instructor's demonstration.'

He gave a small, reluctant shrug. 'OK—if you insist.'

Settling himself on his board, he paddled off, further out, while Jassy collapsed gratefully on hers and allowed the sea to carry her back to the beach.

She sank down on the bottom step, just before her exhausted legs gave out under her, rolling her hood back to release her hair with a little groan of relief. She closed her eyes for a few moments as the mind-blowing fatigue washed through her, then, as she opened them again, she realised that, alongside her, a little knot of spectators had gathered and were looking out to sea. Shading her eyes with her hand against the low sun, she peered out and saw Alain, a tiny silhouette, black against the dazzling silver.

He was sweeping in towards the shore, and as she took in that long fluid movement, seeming almost to hang between the sky and the sea, her eyes widened in astonishment. She'd guessed that he was a good surfer, but not that he was superb. The sea seemed to have no power over him: one moment he was pirouetting the board like a ballet dancer, the next he was playing the waves, teasing them as though he were a matador.

The crowd on the esplanade were greeting his

graceful gyrations with low murmurs of approval and another, lesser man might have been showing off to them—or at least to her. As she watched spell-bound, though, Jassy knew instinctively that he was totally oblivious to everything beyond himself, completely absorbed by the exhilaration of what he was doing, and little by little his sheer physical, animal pleasure transmitted itself to her.

At last, though, after one final spectacular swooping run, he carried on in with the surf and waded through the shallows to the steps. He towered over her, black against the flaring evening sky, then pushed back his hood to ruffle his flattened hair.

As he gazed down at her, his eyes still alight, her insides gave a peculiar sideways lurch and, appalled, she thought suddenly, Oh God—no! Don't let me.

Then, with another sick jolt, It's too late—I've fallen for him!

CHAPTER SIX

'ALAIN—Alain Deville! It just had to be!'

A man detached himself from the group of onlookers and came across to them. Jassy, still caught up in the maelstrom of her emotions, could only stare blankly at him, although the periphery of her mind registered that Alain was not over-pleased to see the newcomer.

'Hello, Philippe.' Then, with obvious reluctance, 'Jassy, meet an old schoolfriend of mine, Philippe Vautier.'

She managed to climb to her feet, smile and put out her hand. As he took it, the man said, 'I hope you enjoyed your surfing lesson, *mademoiselle*.'

She could still barely focus on him, but even so it was absolutely vital that Alain should not suspect in the slightest her inner turbulence, so she managed a sketchy mock grimace, 'Oh, dear, were you watching?' And when he nodded, smiling, she added, 'Well, it *was* my first lesson!'

'You have *la bonne chance, mademoiselle*.'

'Lucky? Oh, yes, Alain——' somehow she got out his name without a tremor '—is a very good teacher, very patient—he only threatened to drown me once!' She even succeeded in shooting Alain a sideways grin.

'And to have private lessons from Alain Deville—

97

well——' He broke off, eyeing her shrewdly. 'But he has not told you, has he?'

'*Philippe*!'

Behind her, she heard the exasperation in Alain's voice.

'Told me what, *monsieur*?'

'Why, that he is a former surfing champion of France.'

'What?' Jassy's green eyes widened in total astonishment. 'No,' she said slowly, 'he did not tell me that.'

'Ah, well, he always was a modest——'

'Excuse us, Philippe.' Alain's hand was already under her elbow, steering her firmly up the steps. '*A bientôt.*'

His grip did not slacken as he guided her back to the car, where she willed herself to stand, allowing him to unzip her wet suit, then deftly peel her out of it. She avoided the slightest glance at him, but still every tautly stretched nerve-ending was aware only of his body and the glow of health and animal vitality which came from it. He got out of his own suit, then unlocked the boot and picked up their surfboards.

'Why didn't you tell me?' she demanded.

Caught off balance so completely by the potent mix of her emotions, she took refuge in attack, but Alain merely slid the boards into the car, handed her a towel, then reached out another. She scowled at his back.

'You realise you made me look an absolute idiot back there, don't you?'

But he was briskly towelling his wet hair and only raised one eyebrow in a quizzical look which inflamed her already smouldering temper. Her voice rose another half octave. 'When I asked you if you could surf, you just said that you——'

'Be quiet.' He did not raise his voice, but something in the tone silenced her. 'You are busy making yourself look a fool right now.'

He opened the car door and, very conscious all at once that she was providing a free street show for the late sun-worshippers still basking on the sea wall, Jassy clamped her mouth tight shut and climbed in without another word. Alain slid in beside her.

'Now,' he said quietly, 'I did not tell you because, firstly, it is not of the least importance; secondly, I have a strong suspicion that you consider me an arrogant enough swine already; and thirdly,' his voice was still completely matter-of-fact, 'it will be for my own sake and not for any spurious long-ago glamour, when I have you.'

When I have you—*when*, not if. His total self-assurance rocked her already tottering nerves.

'Yes, you really are an arrogant swine.' She gave a shaky laugh. 'You're so very certain of yourself, aren't you?'

'No. At least, not where you are concerned, Jassy—not at all. But you know as well as I do,' she watched, as though she were someone else, as he took her slim hand, letting it lie in his much larger one, 'that we shall come together, finally. It was there, the spark, even that first afternoon of the will-reading—when I could happily have torn you into little pieces. No,' he frowned, 'before then, that first glimpse of each other on the church steps.'

Jassy snatched her hand away. 'It's not true!' she

flung at him wildly. 'You hated me then, and you still do—you must do.'

But his highly tuned radar must have picked up her inner uncertainty, for he leaned towards her and, taking one of the damp curls which hung down by her face, twirled it round and round his finger.

'D-don't. Please,' she said huskily, willing herself to look straight ahead past his right shoulder, 'I don't want you to.'

But he only gave a soft chuckle, then, with a last gentle tug at the curl, released it. 'Well, if you say so. But we shall see.'

He bent forward and switched on the ignition. 'But you can relax—for two or three weeks, at least, I have to go back to New York—I left a desk full of unfinished business there—and then on to London and Paris. And so, for the moment at least, *ma chère* Jassy, the heat is off.'

And sure enough, over the next three weeks Jassy heard nothing from him. When he dropped her at the Villa Chantal, she had half expected him to invite himself in, but, in response to her mumbled thanks for the lesson, he had only given her a rather enigmatic smile, ordered her not to surf alone while he was away but promised her more lessons when he got back, if she was a good girl. She had been still working out her reaction to that when, with a casual wave and a flurry of gravel, he roared off down the drive.

Jassy had tried to fill in her time, but it wasn't easy. There was little for her to do in the villa, which was so efficiently managed by Céline, and so she spent much of her days on the beaches. But she had devoted so much time to Armand these last few months that she had not made any friends in Biarritz, and now, surrounded by lively groups of holiday-makers—or, at least, couples—for the first time in her adult life she felt very much on her own.

In any case, she had decided ruefully, a life of idle luxury didn't suit her. In spite of Alain's gloomy warnings, she escaped from her loneliness into happy daydreams of turning the Villa Chantal into a flourishing clinic—it would, she thought, be extremely satisfying to prove him wrong—but August was such a dead month, with everyone grimly hellbent on enjoying *les grandes vacances*, that any such scheme would have to wait until at least September.

And so, despite all her strenuous efforts to blank off her mind with other things, her thoughts would keep returning in small circles to Alain, almost as though he was at the centre of her mind. . . Where was he now. . .? What was he doing. . .? And, endlessly, the even more infuriating, Did he ever think of her?

Above all, she had gone over and over that moment of terrifying self-revelation on the steps at the Côte des Basques. All that night, she had tossed wakefully in bed, still stunned—and shamed—by the violence of her feelings, which, like thrusting a torch into dry brushwood, had erupted in an instant in a blaze of sexual longing. And that was all it was, of course—her feelings for him were purely physical, brought on, like sunstroke, by too much exposure to an attractive, virile man. She'd told herself that next morning, and so many times since that now she knew it was true.

And she also knew that that blaze had to be ruthlessly extinguished, or she would be caught up in it and utterly consumed. To get involved with a man like Alain, who in spite of regarding her as an unscrupulous gold-digger had proposed marriage, for the most cynical of reasons, would be sheer madness. She had been able to see the break-up of two relationships in the past with just a little heartache and some tears, but all her instincts for self-preservation told her that with Alain it would not be tears, it would be her heart's blood that would be wrung from her.

And yet. . . When I have you. . . Her resolve quailed before that overweening self-assurance, but then she told herself that she was old enough to stand up to a hundred Alain Devilles, that, if it came to the crunch, she would just have to convince him that there was no future for either of them in any relationship beyond the most formal one of being boardroom partners in Parfumerie Deville.

He had said he would be away for two or three weeks. Well, three weeks had gone now, and it was the weekend of August the fifteenth—*le Quinze Août*—when the entire country was on holiday. Jassy had the villa to herself: Céline was in Pau visiting her married daughter, whose first child was due at any moment, and she had given the rest of the servants the weekend off.

Jassy had hoped that a couple of days on her own might give her the chance to sort out her muddled thoughts about her future. She might also be able to get on top of the edginess that she had increasingly been feeling, and which for several days she had told herself had been brought on only by the close, humid weather. A violent thunderstorm the previous afternoon, though, had cleared the air but done nothing for the strange, restless mood that gripped her.

But after breakfast on the Saturday she found herself wandering aimlessly from room to room, conscious of every sound she made echoing through the empty house, until finally she retreated to the pool, where she stretched herself out on a padded lounger with a long, cool drink and a book.

Beyond the drive, she could hear the traffic, car horns pipping exuberantly, the shouts of holiday-makers. Everyone in France was obviously having a marvellous time—except herself. How depressing fête days were when one didn't have any family or friends to share them with. Tears of self-pity smarted in her eyes and, angrily picking up her book, she resolutely opened it at page one. : .

Three hours later, having reached page twenty, she was trying to summon up enough energy to go in and prepare herself a tray lunch when the phone rang. A wholly irrational thrill of childish antici-pation went through her, and running across the terrace she snatched up the receiver.

'Mademoiselle Jacinth?'

'Oh—Céline.' Bitter disappointment was sweep-ing through her. 'How is your daughter?'

'Not very well, I'm afraid, *mademoiselle*. The doctor has ordered her to remain in bed, so——' She hesitated.

'You'd like to stay with her? Of course, no problem.'

'But how will you manage?'

'Perfectly well, Céline,' Jassy said firmly. 'And look, you must stay as long as you want to—you're not to worry about me.'

When she finally put down the receiver, Jassy leaned against the wall for a moment, then abruptly straightened up and went through to the kitchen. She sawed off the crusty end of a *baguette* and stood absently gnawing it. . . Perhaps, after all, it would be better to go back to England, pick up the threads of her life there again. She could put the villa on the market, and sell her shares to Alain—give him what he so badly wanted, she thought wryly.

This time, when the phone rang, she hesitated, listening to its insistent ring before finally going to answer it.

'Jassy?'

'Y-yes.' Her heart was already doing painful gymnastics against her ribs at the familiar deep voice.

'I was about to hang up. I thought you must have gone out.'

'Oh, no. Town's so busy I decided to stay put.' Her stomach was looping the loop, but she was delighted to hear her cool, even offhand voice. 'Are you in New York?'

A low laugh came down the wire. 'Heavens, no! I'm here in Biarritz.'

How strange. The involuntary thought leapt into her mind—he was actually here, perhaps half a mile away from her, and yet her intuition, sixth sense— nothing had let her know.

'You've had a good trip?'

'Yes, I must tell you about it. But I was ringing to say, are you planning on watching the *spectacle pyrotechnique* tonight?'

'The——?' Temporarily, her excellent French seemed to have deserted her.

'You know, the fireworks display on the beach.'

'Oh, of course. I'd forgotten.' In fact, every hoarding and lamppost in Biarritz had been plastered with posters for days. 'No, I didn't think I would. Céline said that it gets very crowded, coaches coming in from miles around, and anyway——'

'Anyway?' he prompted.

'Oh, nothing.'

She'd been about to say that it wouldn't be much fun to go down on her own, but that might have seemed as if she were——

'Good. In that case you can come round to my place. There will be no crowds, I promise you.' There was a faintly ironic undertone. 'My house looks out over the bay, so you'll have a grandstand view.'

Her first reaction was pure terror, but a blunt refusal would only betray this to him, so she babbled inanely, 'I didn't know you had a house in Biarritz— surely a fancy-free type like you would just settle for a bachelor pad somewhere?' Even as she spoke, the sudden realisation came to her that she knew nothing, or next to nothing, about Alain.

She heard him chuckle. 'Of course I have a house here. I suppose you thought I inhabit a lair, from which I emerge, wolf-like, to snatch up hapless young females.'

'Something like that—yes.' Little pig, little pig, let me come in.

'So do come, Jassy.'

'Well, I'm not——'

'Look. This is a family weekend, right? You are on your own, so am I. I'm sure you don't want to inflict a solitary Fifteenth of August on me, or even worse, think of me forced in desperation to invite Tante Monique and her brood. So you must take pity on a poor, lonely man.'

'Oh dear, how tragic!' She was even able to echo his mock-serious tone. 'But I'm sure there are a dozen women in Biarritz who'd be glad to oblige.'

'Oh, a dozen at least—but it's your company I want.'

'I'm truly gratified, but——'

'That's settled, then. I will pick you up at seven— that will give us plenty of time to eat before the display.'

And before she could reply, the phone went dead. Slowly Jassy replaced the receiver, then, catching sight of her reflection in the mirror, flushed and brilliant-eyed, she fiercely wiped her face clear of its inane smile and went back to the kitchen.

As her hands performed the mechanical tasks of slicing tomatoes and washing lettuce, her mind was free to range forward to the evening ahead. The firework display was reputed to be just about the most spectacular in France, and, after all, it would be much more pleasant not to be alone for the whole of this holiday weekend. And if Alain attempted to turn it into anything other than a social occasion— well, it would be an ideal chance to show him, once and for all, that she was perfectly able to stand up to any of his wiles.

In the late afternoon, she had a leisurely bath, then shampooed and conditioned her hair, afterwards drying it in the sun until it shone like a darkly glowing halo of fire around her delicate oval face. Then she sat at her dressing-table, studying herself intently.

There was little need for make-up—over the past few weeks she had managed to achieve a very light gold tan, and besides, this evening, there was a wild-rose flush on her cheeks, while her eyes gleamed deep emerald. So she contented herself with just the faintest touch of soft brown eyeliner, a coat of mascara on her long lashes, then outlined her full mouth with a brownish-peach lip-gloss.

What she should wear had cost her an hour of indecision, during which she had removed every outfit from her wardrobe, held it against herself, then discarded it. If Alain took her to an exclusive restaurant for dinner, this dress would be too casual. . . On the other hand, if he had chosen one of the pleasant down-town bistros, this silk skirt and blouse would be far too fancy. He should have told her where they were going. Once more, he had shown precious little consideration, she thought irritably, as she bundled handfuls of clothes away again.

Now her final choice lay on the bed. Sleeveless, with a scoop neckline front and back, and a barely outlined waist, it was a simple sliver of a dress, in a fine crinkly black polyester, which looked exactly like matt silk. It had been a chainstore buy just before she'd left England, though no one could possibly suspect that, she thought. She put on the black lacy briefs and strapless, cunningly wired, matching bra, which she had bought in Nouvelles Galeries a few weeks before, and finally slid into the dress, revelling in the cool, sensuous feel of the material against her skin.

It was the sort of dress which did not need a lot of ornament, so she just slipped two slim gold bangles on to her wrist, clipped in her small gold hoop earrings, then stood back to survey herself—though not wholly with satisfaction. Over the past years, she had created a polished, professional woman out of herself, and yet still, in her face, at odd times—including now—underneath the sophistication there lurked a wistfulness, an almost childlike vulnerability. . .

She turned away quickly from the dressing-table, then caught sight of her antique gold locket lying in the glass tray. Perhaps that ultra-plain neckline could do with just a little something. She picked it up and put it round her neck. The fiddly little catch was always awkward, so in the end, shaking her hair out of the way, she bent forward to peer into the mirror. Next moment the locket slipped through her fingers down on to the tray.

He was leaning against the door-jamb, his casual attitude echoed in the grey canvas jeans, loose grey jacket and black fine-knit polo sweater. When their eyes met in the mirror, he straightened up and came in as Jassy, her hands still to her throat, backed away a few steps, the wild, unreasoning joy which had flooded through her at the first sight of him ebbing away to a wary tenseness.

'Forgive me if I frightened you.' The apology was smoothly said, but she sensed a tautness in him too. 'I rang the bell several times, but there was no one downstairs, so I came on up.'

'No, Céline and the others are all away.' It seemed to be someone else speaking for her.

'Permit me.'

He stooped and retrieved the locket, then, before she could move a muscle, he had encircled her neck with the fine gold chain and, sliding his hands across her throat, hooked it up. She felt his warm fingers brush against her skin, his breath stirring the silky tendrils of hair on her forehead, but she could not look at him.

He lifted her curls clear of the chain, then, as he stepped back, she finally managed to look up. Their eyes met, and something seemed to shimmer in the air between them, hang for a moment, then fade, as they both jerked themselves free. Simultaneously, as Jassy turned away, blindly fumbling her feet into her black high-heeled sandals, Alain picked up her small black clutch bag and held it out to her.

'I'm ready,' she murmured.

When he gestured her past him she led the way downstairs without a backward glance. Once outside, he took the key from her and locked the front door, but then, when she held out her hand for it, he shook his head and slid it instead into his jacket pocket.

'You'll lose it in that ridiculous little bag—I'll keep it for you.'

In silence, she followed him down the steps to the car. Instead of opening the door for her, though, he turned to her.

'I really must tell you,' again, behind his smooth words, she wondered if he were wholly at ease, 'how beautiful you look, Jassy.'

Before she could move, he lifted her right hand and, turning it over, softly kissed it in an elegant, old-fashioned gesture. When he lifted his head, he gave her a little smile.

'You are wearing Chantal.'

'Oh well,' she was trying desperately to recover her own vanished poise, 'if I'm going out for the evening with a Deville, the least I can do is wear one of the family perfumes.'

'But what a sacrifice, when you do not care for it.' He too, it seemed, was grateful to seek refuge in banter.

As they drove away, she asked, 'Where are we going to eat? I'm amazed you could get a reservation anywhere in town tonight.' Although, of course, a little thing like the Fifteenth of August would be no obstacle for Alain Deville——

'Precisely. And that's why we're eating at my villa. If you have no objection, of course.'

His slanting glance was daring her to protest, but she kept an iron grip on the panic that was fizzing through her again and only said primly, 'Of course not. I'm sure that will be very pleasant.'

CHAPTER SEVEN

ALAIN swung off the Avenue de l'Impératrice between a pair of stone pillars which proclaimed the Villa Atalanta. He pulled up at the end of the gravelled drive, cut the engine, then turned to Jassy with that same oblique smile.

'Welcome to the wolf's lair.'

Jassy got out and stood, slowly surveying the expansive façade of the villa.

'Oh, Alain.' She clasped her hands together in an instinctive gesture. 'It's beautiful!'

Her eyes ranged over the peach-washed walls, chocolate-brown shutters, wrought-iron balconies and on up to the steep red-tiled roof. Across the entire width of the front ran a pergola, its wooden supports smothered in wisteria and a rampant blue-starred plumbago, while the house itself was half covered with green creeping ivy.

Beyond the drive were formal flower-beds filled with petunias and geraniums, and beyond them again was a pool with a single jet of water playing into a weathered stone basin. A thick screen of plane trees and greenish-blue cypresses completely enclosed the grounds, giving a feeling of total seclusion in the middle of the bustling town.

She turned to him. 'It's absolutely perfect. What a lovely home!'

He shrugged. 'Well, more of a house than a home,

I'm afraid—these days I seem to spend very little time here. But I'm glad you like it. Come on inside.'

He led the way up the steps and she followed him, conscious of the peculiar little flutterings inside her, brought on, she knew, because for the first time she was actually on his private territory. The spacious hall was tiled in cream and black, with a wide cream-painted staircase, and she just had time to take in the wall hangings in dark green watered silk before he ushered her on into an elegant dining-room. He strode across to a pair of french windows and flung them open to reveal a tiled patio, where dinner for two was already laid at one end of a glass-topped bamboo table.

'Now, you sit here,' he pointed to a low deeply padded armchair, 'while I get us a drink and check on the meal.'

'You mean *you're* cooking it?'

He shook an admonishing finger at her. 'Don't look so alarmed! Marie has prepared it and all I have to do is follow her *extremely* detailed instructions. She and Albert—they are the couple who run the house for me—have gone down to Hendaye for the holiday.'

All the servants in Biarritz seemed to be on the move this weekend, Jassy thought involuntarily. So they really were completely alone this evening, without even the safety barrier of domestics between them. But she thrust away this disturbing thought and went to stand up.

'Let me help you, then.'

'Certainly not.' He pushed her—fairly gently—back down into the chair. 'You're my guest this evening, and anyway, I am quite capable of serving a meal without burning it or throwing it all over the kitchen floor. So, no more female chauvinism, please. Now, that drink.'

As he disappeared into the house, Jassy realised that she was sitting bolt upright, her hands clutching the bamboo arms of her chair as though it were a life-raft. Willing herself to sink back into its up-holstered comfort, she let her eyes roam past the delicate outline of the cypresses to the sweep of sea, enclosed on one side by the headland with its stark white lighthouse, on the other by the hotels and beaches of Biarritz, with the hazy blue outline of the Pyrenees beyond.

'You see what I mean about a grandstand view?'

Alain had approached silently, like a big cat, and she started at the sound of his voice beside her.

'Yes, it's a wonderful view. I suppose that's Spain down there.' She cursed herself inwardly for sound-ing so formal and ill at ease, and in an attempt at nonchalance she leaned back even further, crossing one leg over the other.

'That's right. On a clear day, you can see as far as San Sebastian.' His voice too, seemed ever so slightly stilted.

He set down the tray he was carrying, poured two long pale orange drinks, dropped a couple of ice cubes into each, then passed her one and sat down in the chair beside her. She sniffed at it cautiously.

'Don't look so suspicious! It's vodka and orange, but I promise you it is much more orange than vodka. I certainly don't want you—what is the word?—legless by the end of this evening.' He raised his glass. '*A votre santé*, Jassy.'

'*A votre santé.*'

She echoed his formal toast, then looked up at him. Their eyes met directly for the first time since they had left her villa and she felt the tension uncoil and wreathe itself like smoke around them.

'Yes, I wouldn't want to miss the fireworks.' Her voice was still brittle and she went on quickly, 'I suppose they let them off from down there?'

He nodded. 'From the Grande Plage, but that won't be until about eleven, when it's really dark. So we have plenty of time to eat before then.'

He sat back in his chair, his cool grey eyes, slightly narrowed against the setting sun, studying her, and she stared down at her drink, slowly swirling it round and round until the ice cubes surfaced and then disappeared. Oh, why had she ever been so crazy as to agree to this invitation? One more solitary evening with a book would have been so much preferable—so much safer.

'I owe you an apology, Jassy.'

'Oh?' His words jerked her out of her thoughts and she looked up at him uncertainly. 'An apology? For what?'

'For my unpardonable behaviour towards you.'

'When?'

He grimaced. 'Have there been so many occasions?'

'Well, no,' she began hesitantly.

'I mean when we first met—the day of Armand's funeral.'

Her eyes flew to his and she saw there the same

consciousness that she knew must be in her own,
roused by the memory of those disturbing words. . .
'It was there, the spark, even that first afternoon of
the will-reading. . . No, before then. . .on *the
church steps*. . .'

But then he went on swiftly. 'At the Villa Chantal,
when the others had left——'

'No, please,' she broke in. 'It was quite under-
standable. I'm sure that, in your situation, I'd have
felt exactly the same.'

But he shook his head firmly. 'It was quite
unforgivable.'

'You mean,' she managed a little smile, 'you don't
any longer believe that I'm a——'

'A cheap little gold-digger,' he cut in almost
brutally. 'No, I do not, Jassy.'

But she barely heard him, for the sheer joy which
was unfolding inside her like golden flower petals.

'Why have you changed your mind?' she asked
slowly.

'I did not know you then—but now I do. At least,'
he went on reflectively, 'I know you better. I think
that, like one of those Russian dolls, there are many
Jassy Powers, and I do not yet know all of them by
any means. One day, perhaps——' He smiled at
her, letting the words hang in the air between them.
'But yes, Armand, as so often, was wiser than the
rest of us.'

Ridiculously, Jassy felt as if she was about to burst
into tears, and to recover herself she bent forward,
reaching for her bag.

'Talking of Armand, I almost forgot.' She was
fumbling in it. 'Maurice came to see me the other

day. He's retired now—in fact, he only stayed on for your uncle, of course. You remember Armand left him some of his effects? Well, among them he found this, and I thought you'd like to have it.'

As she held out the photograph to him, she glanced down, seeing again the two swim-suited figures—a wiry, twenty-years-younger Armand, his arm draped affectionately round a tall, dark-haired lad.

'It's you, I think.'

Alain reached forward, then sat back to study it, holding it between his long fingers.

'Yes, it's me,' he said at last. 'Good heavens—I must have been about fifteen. I was staying with him at the villa. We'd been surfing, I remember—he taught me, you know.' He slipped it into his pocket, then looked across at her with a lop-sided smile. 'Thank you, Jassy. I'm glad to have it. Now,' he uncoiled his length from the low chair, 'time to eat, I think. If you'd like to come to the table, I'll fetch the soup.'

He came back with a tureen and, setting it down, removed the lid. 'You like *potage cressonnière*?'

'Oh yes. Mmm, it smells delicious!'

She watched as he took up the long-handled silver spoon and ladled some of the delicate green-flecked watercress soup into the brown pottery bowl in front of her. He who sups with the devil needs a long spoon. . . From nowhere, the old saying leapt into her mind. Devil. . . Deville—— Did the same apply? Almost certainly. The hysterical little giggle which had bubbled up inside her died an abrupt death, and, lowering her head, she began to eat.

'More soup?'

'No, that's fine, thank you.'

He cleared away and returned with a tray of silver serving dishes of grilled tomatoes, green peas and baby sautéed potatoes, together with a roast leg of lamb encased in golden puff pastry.

'Help yourself to vegetables.'

Handing her a plate, he carved thick slices of lamb, releasing the fruity aroma of stuffing from the centre, then poured two glasses of red wine. They ate in silence for some time, but it was not an easy silence. Alain did not seem disposed to speak, and Jassy, though increasingly conscious that the only sounds were of knives and forks on china, shied away from any attempt at meaningless small talk.

Dusk was settling around them and Alain abruptly produced a box of matches from his pocket, and leaned across to the centre of the table to light the small candles which were floating among pink carnation heads in a cut-glass bowl. Just as he lit the last one, the match burnt down to his fingertips and he hurled it across the garden with a smothered exclamation.

As, minute by minute, the dusk deepened, Jassy could feel herself absorbing his edgy mood through every pore in her skin. Beyond the little glow of light it was now nearly dark and she felt almost as though they were suspended, barely breathing, in that golden circle, waiting for—something.

She sneaked a covert glance at him and saw the line of his lashes, casting a shadow across his high cheekbones. There were fine-etched lines of strain around his eyes and his lips were compressed in a weary tautness that she had never seen before. The easy grace, the almost lazy self-assurance that had marked him until now, seemed to have vanished and there was an air of immense fatigue about him.

'You've been working too hard while you've been away.' The words were blurted out before she could hold them back.

'What?' He seemed to be jolted out of his abstraction and smiled briefly. 'Oh, I always do. But yes, it's been a difficult time.'

'Tell me about it.'

'I suppose that, as a thirty-per-cent Deville shareholder,' in the tiny flickering flames his eyes glinted silver-grey, so that she was not sure whether he was mocking or teasing, 'you should be brought up to date on our affairs.'

'Well, you did promise to tell me about it, didn't you? How did it go in New York?'

'All right, finally. In fact, I think we've made quite a breakthrough.'

He seemed to be making an effort at last, so she pressed on. 'How do you mean?'

'Before Armand died, I'd been involved in negotiations with Brannan International—you know, the hotel chain—and I took them up again. They're a pretty tough crowd to do business with, but we've worked out a deal to supply all their hotel bedrooms world-wide—and that's a hell of a lot of bedrooms—with a specially designed range of our toiletries. Shampoo, conditioner, shower gel, soap—perfumes in the luxury suites, all that kind of thing, gold-wrapped and with the Deville insignia. Apart from anything else, with the kind of guests they attract it will be really good publicity for us.'

'That's great,' she enthused. 'Congratulations.'

'Thank you.' He inclined his head slightly.

'And you've also been in London and Paris?'

'Yes. Paris most of the time. We run our selling from there and I'd made up my mind to fire our head of marketing.' When she looked up at him, shocked by his casual tone, he grinned unapologetically. 'Well, as you yourself pointed out at the board meeting—so very tactfully, of course,' she had the grace to look abashed, 'we desperately need new blood in that area. But in any case, he beat me to it. He's taking a job with one of our rivals—and good luck to them.'

He gathered up the empty dishes and plates and went back inside again, but Jassy, every nerve-end in her twitching, was quite unable to sit still. She fidgeted with her cutlery, then bent forward, her chin on her hand, flicking at the little floating candles with her finger, until two of them collided and then sank with a splutter of hot wax.

Unable to sit a moment longer, she pushed back her chair and began pacing up and down the terrace—twenty paces one way, twenty paces back— then stood, hugging her arms to her, looking out at the lighthouse, a pale white blur on the headland, with its beam of light sweeping rhythmically across the ink-black waves. There was something hypnotic about that monotonous swathe of light and, barely aware of what she was doing, she walked down the lawn as though drawn towards it.

'Jassy.'

Startled, she turned and saw Alain standing in the doorway, but he made no move to come to her, and she went slowly back to her chair.

Her napkin was lying on the ground and he stooped to pick it up, but when she held out her hand for it he merely dropped it on the table beside her. He pushed towards her a china pedestal dish, piled with small golden apricots, and, taking one, she bit into its rosy-orange flesh.

'Mmm, delicious—it's still got the warmth of the sun on it.'

'Yes. Albert grows them on that wall down there—along with peaches and nectarines. They're over for this year now, of course, but perhaps next year——' He left the sentence unfinished.

And just where would she be next year? Unable to contemplate that question, or to meet his gaze, which she knew was on her, Jassy reached forward and took another apricot. Somehow, she just had to shake herself free of this cat-on-a-hot-tin-roof mood that was threatening to take her over completely. She only felt safe when they were on that totally neutral no-man's-land of Parfumerie Deville, so——

'Have you got a replacement to take over the marketing?' she asked.

'Yes. He's young, but we think alike, I believe. I must arrange for you to meet him soon—try bouncing your ideas off him.'

'I'd like that, although I'm not really sure how much help I can be.'

'But you must be sure, Jassy. Think positive, and

together we can give the company the fresh impetus it needs.'

She smiled faintly. 'You mean the power of positive thinking?'

'Exactly. And we're making a start with that new perfume I showed you—that really will be a winner, if we can get the hype right when we launch it.'

'What kind of—hype do you have in mind?'

'Oh, nothing so vulgar as to offend Tante Monique's delicate sensibilities, I promise you,' an ironic smile touched his lips, 'but as you yourself said, we have to update our image if we are to appeal to the woman of today, worldwide.'

'That's right, but,' she wrinkled her brow, 'the woman of today—do you really think you know what she's like?'

'I hope so. She is intelligent, forthright, knows her own mind, tough, but at the same time she is warm and sensual, able to give—and receive—passion, love.'

'Heavens,' Jassy said faintly. 'And do you really think such a paragon exists?'

'Yes, I do. She is rare—unique maybe, but yes, she exists.' After the briefest of pauses he went on, 'And we've got to begin by getting the name right. Call it something like Milady Number 2, and it will sink without trace.'

'So what do you have in mind? Superwoman?'

'No, I think I've come up with something much more fetching than that.'

'Well, tell me, then,' she said irritably. His tantalising tone was beginning to twitch at her already edgy temper.

'What would you say to—Jassy?'

She gaped at him, totally bereft of speech, and then, as if on cue, the lights along the sea front began to flicker and go out.

'Ah, *les pyrotechniques*. Coffee will have to wait, I'm afraid.'

He glanced across at her and, obviously satisfied with the result of his bombshell, allowed his mouth the faintest quirk of amusement, then pushed back his chair and stood up.

'We shall get the best view from the end of the terrace,' he said, and when, still stunned into silence, Jassy sat motionless he put his hands under her elbows and lifted her clean out of the chair.

'You are cold.'

'N-no.' She finally found a breathless facsimile of her own voice. 'I'm all right.'

How could she tell him that, though her skin was covered in goose-flesh, and all at once her teeth were chattering, inside she was burning hot, as though with a sudden fever? But ignoring her protestation, Alain pulled off his jacket and draped it around her shoulders. His body warmth enveloped her and the sleeves softly brushed against her bare arms, making the fine golden hairs prickle, then stand upright.

At the edge of the patio the faint light of the candles was lost and the velvety darkness was all around them. Alain was standing just behind her; his breath was on her bare shoulder and she could feel the heat radiating from him. Her mouth was dry as lime—the tension around and within her was slowly suffocating her. In another moment she must turn and run, though she did not know from what.

Her leg muscles were already tightening, her fingers gripping hard on the balustrade around the terrace, when without warning, from each end of the beach, enormous salvos of rockets leapt whooshing up into the sky to burst open in a volley of explosions over the sea. The very next instant, line after line of huge nebulae of light appeared and came floating down in cascades of purples, blues and greens.

As oohs and aahs and a splatter of applause came from the terraces lining the esplanade, Jassy swung round, her eyes shining.

'Oh, how marvellous!' she gasped, but then, seeing his eyes fixed, not on the last fading glimpse of pale green fire, but on her, she turned away, the blood at her wrist and throat leaping erratically under the skin.

When the final glow faded the darkness was absolute, but then, moments later, trails of red fire streaked up into the sky with a shrill whistling, then flew apart in white flashes and massive, mind-blowing explosions.

Mind-blowing, and yet, as the display continued, Jassy felt no release of her inner tenseness. Rather, the fizzing of the rockets and aerial Catherine wheels mirrored her own volatile insides, so that her body seemed like a bottle of sparkling wine, shaken hard and barely contained from violent eruption.

Silence and total blackness again, then another swish of cannonades. But this time, one rocket appeared suddenly to swing off course and hang right over their heads. As the noise ripped the air like thunder, Jassy, her hands clasped tightly to her ears, ducked in terror and stepped back, colliding sharply with Alain's hard body. Before she could jerk away, he had pulled her to him, into the shelter of his arms, her hands outspread against his chest so that, beneath the black fine-knit sweater, she could feel his heart thumping under her palms.

For half a dozen of those erratic heartbeats they stood, staring at each other, as though indelibly inscribing every feature on their minds.

'Jassy?'

The word shook a little and the throbbing pulse of desire in his voice was the final electric connection of the circuit that had been building in her for days— or weeks. A faint, breathy sigh escaped her and then their lips met in a burning kiss.

There was to be no gentle, sensual foreplay—the time for that had gone, swallowed up in the tension and conflict that lay behind them, so that each clung to the other blindly, as if they had been engulfed by a white-heat blaze of passion which had simultaneously set both of them alight.

Alain snatched off the jacket which he had draped around her, then, putting his hands behind her, ripped apart the long zip which ran from neck to hip of her dress and let it drop at her feet, to be followed swiftly by the flimsy lace bra and pants. As she stood, with her head slightly bowed, one hand to her throat, curls tumbling around her face, the sky was suddenly illuminated by a huge white fireball and her whole body was lit in a phosphorescent glow.

She heard his breath hiss softly. 'Oh God, Jassy, you are the most beautiful thing I have ever seen!'

She looked up and he gave a shuddering little half-laugh, half-sob, before lifting her into his arms, her creamy flesh moulded under his hands. Beside them on the lawn was a deeply cushioned chaise-longue, and together they sank down on to it.

As he leaned over her she put her hands up, tugging ineffectually to pull his sweater free, but he pushed them aside impatiently and swiftly peeled off his clothes himself before coming down beside her, one leg half across hers.

As he took her into his arms again, the smell, the potent maleness, running through his every vein like a powerful aphrodisiac, she tried to pull him down to her, but he trapped both her hands in one of his, then, raising them to his mouth, turned one palm up, biting into its soft pad.

The scent of him, the touch of him. . .bare flesh against bare flesh. . .the sensual nipping feel of his teeth were setting up spiralling psychedelic patterns in her brain. She moaned, turning against him, and he moved across her, her tender flesh yielding beneath his surge.

As he thrust home, she took him joyfully into her, feeling the long, slow thrust deep inside her body. Around them, all at once, the sky was lit by gigantic comets of flame, their tails spinning off, to cascade down to earth in enormous golden chrysanthemum petals. But, caught up in their own bodies, reaching out to one another's souls, they were barely aware of that coldly glittering fire, the last, fading streaks still hanging in the air like pale silver tinsel.

The powerful, savage rhythm was building inexorably inside them, until they clutched at one another,

their hands slippery with sweat. Above their heads,
one final salvo of rockets leapt skyward again,
peaked, then fell back with slow reluctance towards
the inky sea in showers of white stars. Simultaneously, the building spiral inside Jassy shattered,
flinging her first up into that star-spangled sky, then,
as other, even more brilliant stars burst in her mind,
she was hurtled earthwards again.

CHAPTER EIGHT

JASSY opened her eyes at last. Alain's head was resting on her shoulder, a strand of black hair tickling her cheek. Very gently, she brushed it aside, but he roused, lifting his head to look down at her. In the intense darkness his face was a pale blur; only his eyes had a strange, silver-grey gleam.

'Oh, Jassy!'

'Yes?' It was barely a whisper, and he laughed softly.

'Nothing. Just—oh, Jassy.'

The night wind stirred around them, making her shiver. He caught the slight movement and instantly got to his feet, holding out his hands to her.

'Come. We cannot stay here.'

Raising her to her feet, he held her to him, their bodies blending together in perfect strong-soft harmony. But then he loosed her and, taking up his jacket, which was lying in a crumpled heap at their feet, helped her into it, then slid into his canvas jeans.

'Are you taking me home?' she murmured.

'Of course not. I am taking you where you have belonged since the first time we met.'

And scooping her up into his arms, he carried her into the house, through the shadowy hall and up the curving staircase. He pushed open a door with his shoulder and set her down on a softly carpeted floor.

As he flicked down a switch, Jassy looked round her. The wall lights illuminated a large room with beautiful antique furniture, its dark polished finish perfectly set off by the pale blue Oriental rug which covered the entire floor, and the matching walls.

Since they had entered the room, strange little bubbles of nervousness had been rising in her, and to mask her uncertainty she brushed her hand gently across the wall beside her, feeling the cool silk under her fingers. Running through the pale blue thread was the sheen of gold.

'So this is the wolf's lair.' Still half drowned in the aftermath of passion which had swept over her in a tidal wave, Jassy just about managed a sideways, teasing look.

'Yes,' Alain said, 'this is my lair.' He was watching her, a tiny smile behind his eyes. 'I hope you like it—I had it done a few months ago.'

'It's very nice. I love the wall covering.'

He pulled a face. 'An extravagance, I am afraid. I gave it to myself as a birthday present. It is Indian sari silk which was specially imported. And that reminds me——' he reached out from a cupboard a robe made of the same shimmering blue-gold silk '—this was run up from the left-overs. Take off that jacket—fetching though it looks on you,' he gave her a provocative grin which made him look boyish all of a sudden, 'and put this on.'

'Oh—thank you.'

Her voice, all at once, sounded terribly stilted and, taking the robe from him, she quickly turned her back before slipping off the coat and fumbling herself into it. Still not facing him, she began awkwardly smoothing down the lovely silk. But what a fool she was! After the intensity of their fevered lovemaking in the garden—to be suddenly overcome by shyness, like a young girl.

She turned round at last and when she lifted her drooping eyelids to look at him, he was watching her, a strangely tender half-smile lurking in his eyes. He crossed the room to her and firmly removed her hands, which were fiddling with the towelled knot of the robe, and raised them to his lips.

'Please—don't look like that, my sweet Jassy,' he murmured against the back of her hand, then, still holding her, led the way into the bathroom which opened out of his room.

'Would you like a hot bath?'

'Oh, no—though perhaps a shower?'

Still paralysed with that strange shyness, Jassy stood meekly under his hands as he untied the wrap and took it from her. He stripped off his jeans and lifted her into the shower cubicle, then paused, his hand on the switch.

'May I lather you?' There was the faintest note of uncertainty.

'If—if you like,' she said in a little breath, so he opened a wall cupboard and ran his finger along the row of bottles before finally bringing one out.

'This, I think—one of ours, of course.'

That slanting smile again, then he poured some on to the sponge and set the warm water running before very gently beginning to rub the gel-laden sponge all over her, in long, slow movements. The water warming her chill flesh, the spicy exotic perfume, and above all, the sensuous stroking of every part of her body—down, round, between—sent a heavy languor through her until she closed her eyes, shuddering with voluptuousness.

When at last he finished, he held her close to him and turned the shower on full, letting the water pour over their bodies in a warm cascade. Finally he lifted her out, wrapped her in a bath sheet and blotted her all over, then towelled himself dry. His hair was plastered to his skull like a sleek ebony cap; hers lay in wet strands on her shoulders, but when she went to pick up the wall-mounted hairdrier he put his hand out to her.

'No—later.' At the message in his eyes, she felt herself go hot inside. 'You see, I've always had this fantasy about capturing a beautiful, slim, copper-haired water nymph, and now—she is here, wet, coppery hair, and——' slowly, he pulled the bath sheet away from her body '—everything.'

Back in the bedroom, he turned down the heavy, fringed white bedspread, lowered her on to it, then lay beside her. Propping himself on one elbow, he let his eyes travel over her, slowly taking in every delicate curve of her creamy gold flesh. At first, he did not touch her physically, though his eyes burned her flesh, making her tremble.

'You know,' he murmured, 'you are exactly like one of those ripe apricots—warm, golden and luscious.'

He began stroking her, rubbing his curved palm down her shoulder, over her full breasts, across her flat stomach, where a tiny pulse flickered just under the skin. He rested his hand there for a few moments, then went lower still, circling her thighs, brushing to and fro lightly across the soft hair, until deep within her she began to quiver.

Only then did he look up at her, his grey eyes, so often mocking or sardonic, filled with such naked yet tender desire that her insides lurched and turned to water. Afraid that he would see the tell-tale expression mirrored in her own eyes, she turned her head away and put one arm up to shade them.

'Please, Alain,' she said huskily, 'put off the light.'

'Oh, no.' He brushed her lower lip in a butterfly kiss. 'I want to see you.'

Slowly, inexorably, ignoring her muffled pleas, he pulled her arm away from her face, holding it by the wrist. 'This time, I want to see the proud, beautiful, wilful Jassy surrender—I want to see that look in those lovely green cat's eyes—and, most of all, I want to see you come alive for me.'

And lowering his head, he began to taste her with his mouth and tongue, feasting on the richness of her body until, lost to everything but her blind need of him, she writhed under his touch, crying out his name in wild, incoherent sobs. . .

'*Chérie*.'

The word was echoing softly in Jassy's subconscious, gradually penetrating the layers of sleep, until she stirred. Her heavy eyes flickered, then opened, and she registered first that this bedroom ceiling above her head was not her own, second that there was a loaded tray by the bed, and third, in almost the same instant, that Alain, in black towelling wrap, was sitting on the bed beside her.

'Lazybones,' he mocked softly.

'Mmm.' She lay, smiling drowsily up at him as, twining his finger into one of the copper curls that tumbled on the pillow, he tugged it gently.

'Wake up. I've made us some breakfast. After all,' he shot her a glinting smile, 'we never did have that coffee I promised you last night.'

She blushed as the memory of the night came flooding back, but he put his finger on her lips. 'No, Jassy—no shame, no regrets. Now, eat—it's nearly eleven o'clock.'

'*Eleven*!' Her eyes flew open in astonishment. She never slept late.

'Afraid so. You slept through the dawn chorus, the church bells, a helicopter hovering over the beach—and me, sitting here, watching you. Still, when you look so beautiful,' his eyes ranged over her face and outstretched body, half hidden in a tangle of sheet, 'all is forgiven.'

Plumping up the pillows behind her, he hoisted her up unceremoniously, then broke open a croissant and buttered it.

'Strawberry jam?'

'Please.'

As she watched his hands perform the task with neat efficiency, Jassy remembered. Those hands— gentle, strong, giving, demanding by turns—coaxing from her responses which she had never before dreamed herself capable of, and which had at last, in the early hours, left her totally sated, spent——

'Black or white coffee?'

'Could I have tea, do you think?'

Alain rolled his eyes in mock horror. '*Les anglais*! Ah well, if you must. Indian, China, black, white, lemon?'

'Indian—white—no sugar, please.'

He came back with a silver teapot and, sitting down beside her again, poured the tea. He was frowning in absolute concentration—she'd never met a man quite like him before, a man who could absorb himself so completely into whatever he was doing at a particular moment: running a board meeting, surfing, or something so trivial as preparing a simple breakfast. And yet there was not the least hint of prissiness in him, rather of absolute control of himself.

He was unshaven; his mouth, normally so cynical, world-weary, was soft and relaxed; and his hair, still tousled with sleep, fell untidily forward over his brow, giving him an endearing, even vulnerable quality. It set up in her a strange, wholly new sensation, almost like a physical ache, and she found herself yearning to reach out and smooth it away.

But she had revealed quite enough of herself to him already through the night, so when he handed her the cup, she primly pulled up the sheet across her breasts.

'By the way, I like the designer stubble,' she remarked.

Pulling a rueful face, he rasped his hand across his dark chin. 'Yes, a real Deville special, I'm afraid. I usually shave twice a day.'

He passed her the croissant and they ate in companionable silence.

'Now, up you get,' he said at last. 'We have to go out.'

'Oh, no—I don't want to go out. Please, Alain!' she pouted, but he held up his hand to silence her.

'Yes. I am taking you into town, to buy our lunch.'

'But I shan't want any lunch,' she protested. 'And besides, it's Sunday.'

He picked up the tray. 'No arguments. On the Sunday of the Fifteenth, everyone goes into town. You shall see.'

When he had gone, Jassy pushed back the sheet and slowly got up. Her whole body was filled with a delicious, aching languor, while under her soft skin slight puffy marks showed where Alain had held her.

Catching up her bra and pants, which Alain must have brought in from the garden, together with her dress, she went through to the bathroom. When she had showered, she leaned against the basin, staring at herself. Her eyes, brushed underneath with dark shadows, shone with muted green fire; her full lips, swollen from his kisses, were parted in a tremulous smile, and on her face was an expression she had never seen before. More than a glow, it held a warm, secret fulfilment.

Oh, Jassy, what have you done? she asked herself, almost fearfully. All her resolve not to let herself get involved in any way—much less a full-scale affair— with this dangerous man, broken into fragments. . .

She stood, gnawing at her lower lip, then, No. No shame, no regrets. And then, one day, when it was over, as, inevitably, it would be, she'd be able to walk away from him, quite undamaged.

'Yes, I shall,' she said aloud, and went back to the bedroom.

She picked up her black dress, then paused. Fine for a dinner for two, it was hardly suitable for a Sunday morning in town.

'What's wrong?' Alain was standing in the doorway, watching her quizzically.

'I can't wear this dress, not this morning.'

'Why not?'

'Well, what will people think?'

'They will no doubt think that you have just come from a night of love in my arms. But does that worry you?'

She managed to meet his look unwaveringly. 'No—no, it doesn't,' and slipped into the dress.

But then, as she reached behind her for the zip, she realised that it had been completely wrecked.

'I really can't wear it. Look!' She turned round for his inspection.

'Hmm. Yes, you're right. Sorry.' He gave her a wry grimace. 'Never mind, though, you shall have half a dozen new dresses instead, I promise. But for now——' He frowned at her consideringly, then, tugging open the bottom drawer in a chest, pulled out a couple of garments and tossed them at her.

'I bought these in California last year. If you use this,' he handed her a narrow white leather belt, 'I should think they will fit you well enough.'

And amazingly, when, rather unwillingly, she put on the lemon and white cotton bermudas and baggy lemon overshirt, he was right.

* * *

Having neatly outmanoeuvred another driver to gain
what appeared to be the last parking space in town,
Alain took off in the direction of the indoor market.
The streets were thronged with people, all in Sunday
best, and obviously out shopping, with bottles of
wine clinking in baskets and long sticks of bread
under their arms. A priest, in festal dress, rode past,
a large bunch of white carnations in his bicycle
pannier.

'That's one of the traditions of this weekend,'
Alain remarked, 'taking flowers to family or—loved
ones.'

By the entrance to the market were some flower
stalls. He stopped beside one and, before Jassy could
prevent him, he had scooped up the entire contents
of a huge tub of multi-coloured gladioli and passed
them to the astonished stallholder.

Five minutes later, with the flowers swathed in
cellophane and white ribbon, he handed over a wad
of notes, then thrust the massive bouquet at Jassy.
She clutched them to her, only just able to get both
arms round them.

'Oh, Alain,' she said exasperatedly, 'one bunch
would have been fine. You never do anything by
halves, do you?'

'That's right,' he agreed cheerfully, but then, at
the meaningful look he gave her, she went scarlet
and retreated hastily into silence.

Inside the market, they queued up at one of the
charcuterie stands, Jassy all too aware of the free
sideshow she was providing as she constantly hitched
up the tall flower spikes into her aching arms. While
she stood at his side, feeling decidedly superfluous,

Alain bought a selection of cold meats and a tray of cooked chicken portions, covered with mayonnaise and decorated with sliced truffles and pistachio nuts.

As they moved from stall to stall, buying bread, pâtés, salad and fruit, Jassy gradually realised that she was thoroughly enjoying the casual intimacy of this impromptu shopping trip with Alain. It was almost as though they were——

She bit off the thought and followed him round the corner to Dodin's *pâtisserie*, then watched in silence as a large gold-beribboned box was produced and paid for.

Once outside, though, she said accusingly, 'It was already ordered, wasn't it?'

'Yes. I telephoned them yesterday.'

'You're doing it again, aren't you—taking me for granted, I mean?'

Anger—and a spasm of panic—were rapidly rising in her, but he merely raised his eyebrows in pained surprise.

'I have told you before, Jassy, a man would be very unwise to assume anything about you. But I happen to be very fond of coffee gâteau, so, if you had insisted on going home last night—well——' he gave an extremely Gallic shrug '—at least I would have had the gâteau to console me.'

As she walked alongside him, struggling to keep up with his long strides, the flowers began to slip yet again. She was hoisting them up, but then, catching the secret twitch of amusement at his mouth, she stopped dead.

'Can you help me, please?' she asked.

'Of course.'

He put down the various boxes on the steps of a church they were just passing, then took the flowers from her. The moment he had them, Jassy snatched up the packages and set off at a rapid rate in the direction of the car, then leaned up against it, her arms folded, to enjoy his slower progress.

After a struggle, he got the boot lid open and dropped the flowers in, then gave her a long look across the car roof.

'That was a sneaky trick.'

'Yes, wasn't it?' she said smugly, but then she caught his eye and the next instant they had both dissolved into helpless laughter.

They were still giggling, like a pair of school-children, when they arrived back at the Villa Atalanta. While Alain unloaded the packages, Jassy carried the flowers into the house.

'Have you got a vase—or ten?'

But he snatched them from her, tossed them on to the pine kitchen table, then, before she could guess what he was going to do, he wheeled round and seized her, lifting her clean off her feet.

'No!' she squeaked, torn between terror and laughter. 'Put me down!'

But he was already carrying her towards the stairs. She just managed to poke one elbow hard into his ribs, before he growled menacingly into her ear, 'I'll teach you to make me look an idiot.'

'Really? How?' she got out breathlessly.

'You'll see.'

And, with her still struggling ineffectually in his arms, he went on up the stairs.

* * *

Later—a long while later—they ate a lazy lunch on the terrace, then took their coffee and liqueurs and lay on padded sun-loungers in the shade of an acacia tree.

A delicious indolence was creeping through Jassy's body and she was already drifting away into sleep, so that she was barely aware of Alain removing her half-empty glass, which was resting on her stomach. . .

'Mmm.'

She stretched like a lazy cat, and, opening her eyes, registered with astonishment that the sun was setting. She turned and saw Alain, propped up on his lounger, a briefcase at his side and an open file on his knees.

'Not working, surely—not on the Fifteenth?' She clicked her tongue reprovingly.

He glanced at her. 'Afraid so, but I've just about finished.'

Shuffling the papers together in the file, he returned them to the case and closed it with a decisive click, then looked across at her again.

'So you're awake—at last!'

He leaned over and took her hand in both of his, brushing his thumb slowly across it.

'Don't look so sad, *chérie*.'

'Was I?'

'Yes, you were. Still no regrets, I hope?'

'No.' And yet, deep inside, there was a kind of aching pain, like toothache, which perhaps was regret. But for what? 'It's just that I was wishing that this weekend could go on forever.' That this magic time, with you holding me in your arms, would never end, she thought, but could not say it.

When he said nothing, though, she went on, 'You know, that we're not fighting. Two whole days and not actually coming to blows.'

Alain smiled wryly. 'True. And let us hope this happy state of affairs continues—at least until tomorrow.'

'Just tomorrow?' She made a little moue.

'I shall have to take you back home then.'

'Oh.' So this time tomorrow she would not be with him. The desolation that was sweeping through her jolted her, yet still she managed a teasing note. 'Surely you're not afraid of shocking Maria and Albert?'

He laughed. 'I should not imagine that they shock that easily. And your reputation, if you care about it, would be perfectly safe with them. But no, I have to go back to Paris tomorrow evening.'

He couldn't go. She couldn't bear to be without him.

'H-how long will you be away?'

'Not long. I shall be back on Thursday, in time to take you to the reception at the Hôtel du Palais.'

Jassy looked blankly at him. 'The reception?'

'Yes. You know, Deville are sponsoring the Pro-Am golf tournament this week and I have to present the prizes.' Of course. She remembered now, the others discussing it at the board meeting. 'I shan't be able to get back for the match itself, but if you'd like to go, I can arrange it with my secretary,' he added.

'Oh, no, thank you, I'm not keen on golf,' she replied automatically.

So he was going to be away for three whole days. . . Tears were filling her eyes, and she turned her head away, to stare hard at the last flame streaks of sunset. Oh God, what was wrong with her? Alain just wasn't the sort of man to want a woman who clung to his knees, weeping, every time he left her for more than ten minutes.

All the same, to her horror, she heard the slight quiver in her voice as she asked, 'Can I come to Paris with you?'

The frown was gone so quickly that she thought she must have imagined it. 'No. Not this time.'

He didn't want her to go. The stark realisation hit her like a blow, but somehow her innate pride must not let him see how much his curt refusal hurt, so she said mock-seriously, 'Of course you realise it's only my thirty per cent shares that I'm worried about—making sure you don't get up to any funny business with them.'

'Jassy.' Alain dropped a kiss on the tip of her nose. 'I would love you to come, believe me. But we shall be very busy, getting on with sorting out the big European sales push that we are planning for the spring.'

We? Sophie Larbaud—she was head of European sales, wasn't she? Alain and the glamorous Sophie, closeted together for hours on end. . .? Oh, for heaven's sake, she was becoming more ridiculous by the minute! And yet, when she remembered that swift, assessing look as Sophie left the board meeting, she could not quite suppress the barest flicker of unease. . .

'Do you have a United States entry visa?'

'What?' She was jerked out of her train of thought. 'Er—oh, yes, I have. I was planning on going to a clinic on the West Coast, but then Armand offered me——'

'Good. In that case, you can come with me to New York when I go on Friday.'

'New York!' She gaped at him. 'Oh, Alain, how wonderful! I'd——'

'I shall be preparing the launch of our new perfume over there, and I want our US advertising agency to meet you. It should help them formulate their campaign, if they meet the original Jassy,' he gave her the barest flicker of a smile, 'in the flesh, as it were.'

But she did not react to his bait—in fact, she was beginning to feel quite overwhelmed. 'You mean you really are going to use my name?'

'But of course. You don't think it was just a subtle seductive ploy, do you? Jassy.' He inflected the name with a sensuous tenderness which made the hairs on the back of her neck prickle. 'It will be quite perfect. Unless——' He broke off, that little frown momentarily creasing his brow again.

'Yes?' she prompted.

'Nothing.' He loosed her hand and stood up abruptly. 'Would you like something to eat?'

'No, thanks. But I would love a swim.' Although she had spent the afternoon in the shade, her body felt tacky with sweat. 'You haven't got a pool?'

'No. With the Atlantic two minutes away, I've never felt the need—and anyway, I prefer the sea. But, now you mention it, there is something I can provide.' He held out his hands to her. 'Come and see.'

To one side of the house there was a small space, enclosed by trellis which was smothered in pink, softly scented climbing roses. A narrow archway led inside, where Jassy saw, set in a tiled surround, a large circular blue bath.

'I fell for hot tubs the first time I was in California,' Alain remarked over his shoulder as he squatted down beside it, dabbling his fingers in the water. 'I switched the heater on earlier in case you wanted to use it. Good, the temperature's fine.'

He pressed a plastic knob on the side and a ring of small underwater lights came on, turning the water a deep sapphire blue, then another switch set the surface heaving and bubbling.

He straightened up. 'I hope you approve.'

'Oh, yes.' Jassy's eyes sparkled with pleasure.

'In you get, then. I shan't be long.'

When he had gone, she slipped out of his shirt and bermudas and perched on the edge, dangling her feet in the blue water, from which steam was gently rising. Bliss! The wavelets lapped invitingly round her, bubbles beating gently at her toes, until she shed her bra and pants and slid right in, with a little gasp of pleasure. Surrendering herself to the water, she lay back, the powerful jets keeping her buoyant, her long hair floating mermaid-like around her.

Alain came back, carrying a bottle and two glasses. Catching her eye, he grinned at her.

'My idea of heaven—or, at least, one of them. Bubbles outside, bubbles inside.'

He put them on the tiles and stood looking down at her. The grin had quite gone and in the subdued light his grey eyes held an expression which she could not quite read, yet which all at once made the breath catch in her throat.

'You know,' he said softly, 'I always thought you were a water nymph, and now, lying there, your hair around you, those bewitching green eyes watching me——' He shook his head slightly and shot her a rueful smile. 'I think I must be turning into an incurable romantic in my old age. What an appalling prospect!'

He half turned away, kicking off his espadrilles, then, as she watched through lowered lashes, he peeled out of his T-shirt and jeans. Bronzed, sleek and lithe as a panther, the long line of thigh and haunch, the hard taut muscles visible just under the skin of his stomach. . . Jassy swallowed and then, as he let himself down into the water beside her, his thigh brushed lightly against hers and she moved away a little.

Uncorking the bottle, he poured it, and as he handed her the slim flute its sides misted in the heat of the bath.

'Pink champagne!' she exclaimed. The precious liquid was foaming over the edge of her glass and she caught the trickle with her tongue, sensuously, like a cat.

'Oh, water nymphs never drink anything else,' he said solemnly, then raised his glass. '*A nous*, Jassy.'

'To us,' she echoed, and was glad that the rush and churn of water masked the uncertainty in her voice.

She took a sip, feeling the icy bubbles go up her nose, then set down the glass and lay back again, her eyes half closed.

'What are you thinking?' Alain's face was very near her.

'Oh, nothing. Just, the sky up there——' she gestured towards the night, intense inky violet above their heads '——those roses all around us——' their rich perfume was running all through her veins like the champagne '——and all this. It's so lush and exotic, like something out of an Eastern fairy-tale.' She gave him a sly look. 'All you need is a silk turban—with a ruby the size of a hen's egg in it, of course—and you'd make a wonderful pasha.'

Alain carefully set down his glass and caught her, under the water, by the hand.

'In that case, come here, my beautiful, intoxicating harem slave.'

Next moment he had pulled her into his arms, his mouth covering hers, his tongue thrusting past her teeth with an urgency that made her senses spin wildly out of control. He gripped her to him, until their slippery limbs seemed to fuse together in a white-hot melt-down.

She was drowning, tossing far out in a sea of wild blue water, and above the bubbles which clamoured in her brain she heard the thunderous beat of her own blood, pounding in her ears.

CHAPTER NINE

JASSY was still upstairs in her room when Alain arrived. She heard the long blast on the horn, then the car door slammed, there were footsteps on the gravel and moments later she caught his deep voice in the hall as he spoke to Céline, who had returned earlier that afternoon.

For three days she had walked, talked, waked, slept—or rather, not slept—this man, her skin, no, her very being, after that final sensual night, so permeated with his scent, the feel of him, that she had barely been conscious of anything but the emptiness of her existence without him. Now, though, he had come back.

A wave of suffocating joy flooded through her, so that she yearned to run downstairs and hurl herself headlong into his arms. But instead, of course, she forced herself to finish tucking in the last stray curl, then take time to survey herself from head to toe in the mirror. Only then did she pick up her black velvet clutch bag, draw a deep breath and walk out of her bedroom.

At the top of the stairs she paused. Alain was almost directly below her, still chatting easily to Céline. He was dressed formally, the black trousers emphasising the slim length of leg, the white jacket setting off his broad shoulders, austere, suntanned features and black hair. She could have stood feasting her eyes on him all night, but as though sensing her presence, he glanced up and she made herself walk sedately down the stairs.

She knew that he watched her all the way down, then, as she reached the hall, he moved to meet her and took her hand, raising it to his lips in a formal gesture.

'Jassy.'

'H-hello, Alain.' Their eyes met over her hand and she gave him a tremulous smile. 'Will I be a credit to Deville, do you think?'

He stepped back, still keeping hold of her hand, and surveyed her, slowly turning her so that he could take in every detail of her appearance as, in the huge gilt mirror opposite, another Jassy Powers seemed to stand, elegant and remote.

The lines of her dress were deliberately simple—sleeveless, a soft cross-over bodice, and a gently flaring skirt—to contrast with the richness of the deep blue silk, which under the subdued lights shaded from peacock through to indigo and violet. Her unruly curls were caught up into a narrow band of black silk, leaving her throat and neck bare, just two or three curls left loose against her cheek.

But it was on the face of that other Jassy that Alain's eyes lingered longest: rather pale, but with eyes like stars, and lit from within by a soft, luminous quality.

'Well?' A smile shimmered across her face and she heard his breath catch.

All he said, very gravely, was, 'I think I can safely

say that you will be a credit to the company,' but she was satisfied.

On the doorstep she turned to the housekeeper. 'Don't wait up, Céline.'

'Very well, *mademoiselle*,' and Jassy caught her indulgent, almost maternal smile.

Alain had said nothing more, though, and as he opened the car door for her she reached up and gently brushed her fingers across his lips.

'Oh, Alain, I've missed you so much!'

She knew she shouldn't say it, that she was betraying her inner self to him, but it came out of its own volition. But, seemingly abstracted, he did not respond, and she allowed herself to be handed into the car.

Swinging himself in beside her, he drove off down the avenue. His silence was damping down her spirits by the second and somehow she had to draw him out of it, so, with forced gaiety, she began, 'I hope you like the outfits I've got for New York. I've been on a bit of a spree, I'm afraid, but I wanted to look every inch a member of the Deville board.' She flashed him an impish grin, but still there was no response. 'And I've bought a guidebook, so if you're too busy, I can——'

'You aren't coming, Jassy.'

'What?' She must have misheard him.

But when she swivelled to stare at him, his face illuminated palely by passing street lamps, he only repeated, with more than a hint of impatience, 'You're not coming.'

The cold finality was like a brutal blow across her face.

'But—but why not?' she said in bewilderment, and he shrugged.

'Something has cropped up unexpectedly.'

Jassy sat watching him, but he made no effort to explain further, and beneath the hurt she could feel anger rising. Yet again he was taking her for granted, expecting her to fall meekly into line with his every whim. This time, though, she was damned if she would.

'Oh, and I shall be in the way, I suppose.'

He kept his eyes straight ahead. 'Let us just say that it is no longer convenient. Another time.'

His voice was ever so slightly constrained, and she frowned, tapping her foot. There was something odd going on here. He was being almost—what was the word?—evasive, no, shifty.

'But I've bought all those clothes!' she wailed.

Alain lifted one shoulder. 'If it is the clothes that are worrying you, forget it, please. I shall of course pay for them.'

'*Oh*!' The shuddering gasp was torn from her. 'You know it isn't that, Alain.'

How could he treat her like this, after all they had——? As she broke off, closing her eyes against the anguish of the images which were invading her mind, a cold, cynical little voice whispered, Very easily. After all, why should you, in the end, have expected anything more than casual cruelty from Alain Deville? A man like him was inevitably going to be casual with women, while as for the cruelty—well, you saw that in his face the first time you met, didn't you? Even so, hot tears were stinging her eyes, blurring the outline of the shops and giving golden haloes to the oncoming headlights.

'Turn the car round.' She spoke in a high, dead voice. 'I'm not coming tonight.'

'I am afraid you are.' His own voice was perfectly level. He, no doubt, had far more experience of scenes like this than she.

'No, I'm damn well not!'

Then, when he made no response, she snatched at the handbrake and wrenched it on so that the tyres screeched, slewing the car round at an angle. With an oath, he righted it and, as horns blared all around them, swung back into the flow of traffic.

'Get it into your head,' he snarled. 'You are expected and, willing or unwilling, you will be there.'

The car swept in through the wrought-iron gates, a gold-braided guard saluting, then up the long drive to pull up alongside the huge glass-canopied entrance. Alain switched off the engine but let his hands still rest on the wheel, one thumbnail picking at the leather seam. Without looking at her, he said abruptly, 'Jassy, I shall take you with me later, I promise.'

'Oh, promises, promises!' she hurled at him bitterly. 'Don't bother, please.'

His lips tightened on an angry retort and he got out, slamming the door. Jassy just had time to pull out a lace handkerchief, pat away a large tear which was threatening to ruin her mascara, then cram it back into her bag, and he was opening her door.

On the steps he stopped, a hand on her arm. 'Just one thing—behave yourself tonight.'

She shook herself free and said between her teeth, 'Don't you tell me how to behave, you—you——'

She bit back the expletive. Her temper was beginning to resemble a kettle coming to the boil and any minute now the lid was going to take off. But, for public consumption at least, she must keep herself under tight control, so she followed him up the steps and in through the swing doors.

Placing his arm round her waist in what looked like an affectionate, even solicitous gesture, but which was in fact a clear warning, his fingers digging into her flesh through the thin silk, Alain led her through the sumptuous, marble-pillared foyer to the Salon Impérial.

The brilliance of the high-ceilinged room almost stunned her, the gilt and crystal chandeliers reflecting off the tall mirror-glass doors. The salon was already full of impeccably groomed guests—this was clearly the in-place tonight for all the Beautiful People, Jassy thought waspishly.

But then, as Alain steered her forward, she tacked a dazzling, empty smile in place and helped herself to a glass of champagne from the tray which a white-gloved waiter was holding. The last time she'd drunk champagne, she and Alain——

He was bending forward, as though to whisper an intimate something in her ear. 'Just one more thing—don't drink too much either.'

'I will drink precisely as much as I want to, thank you,' she hissed. 'You are *not* my keeper!' She paused, then for good measure added venomously, 'Thank God!'

Catching the interested eye of a man standing nearby, she pinned her slipping smile back into place, then deliberately took a long swig at the champagne. As they stood there, stiffly, side by side, she let her eyes range over the long, glittering room, the dove-grey and gilt décor, the half-pillars and crystal wall lights—anywhere but at the man standing at her side.

At the far end, a small stage was set with a table piled with trophies and swathed in banners proclaiming 'Deville Pro-Am Tourney'. Deville, Deville—she was getting sick of the bloody name!

'Alain.' A man clapped him on the shoulder. 'There's someone who's very anxious to meet you. If you would excuse us, *mademoiselle*.'

Before Jassy could even smile and nod, Alain had put down his empty glass on a tray beside them and without so much as a glance at her walked off. She watched him go, threading his way through the throng, until his broad-shouldered figure was lost, but then as her gaze continued to strain after him she suddenly caught sight of Martine's cold eyes fixed on her in a speculative stare.

Of course—she was bound to be here, and no doubt the others as well, but Jassy simply had to keep away from them, for she wasn't at all sure that she could maintain her flimsy façade for long in the face of any close-up scrutiny, from the two female members of the clan in particular.

Setting down her glass, she took another one and downed half of it, then moved further into the room to join an animated group clustered around a man who she realised, with a little thrill of shock, she had last seen singing on stage in a televised spectacular from the Hollywood Bowl. He was, she gathered, one of the 'Am' competitors, and, now that she looked around her, she saw that among the increasingly crowded throng were several faces that she recognised from the glitzy world of show business.

She was just raising her glass to her lips again, when she saw Marcel Ridoux, who had just entered the room and was standing on his own in the doorway. Gratefully she went over to him, they shook hands and she drew him further into the room.

'How are you, Mademoiselle Powers?'

'Oh, I'm fine, absolutely fine.'

'Splendid. I am delighted to hear it.' But she wasn't at all sure that her too eager assurance had fooled this shrewd lawyer's intution, and when she met his eyes she seemed to catch the tail-end of what might even have been a slightly perturbed expression.

'And you are happy at the Villa Chantal?'

'Oh, yes, Céline has been such a great help.'

'But of course. Armand always chose his servants well.' There was a slight pause. 'So you are still decided on remaining here in Biarritz?'

Jassy tilted her chin a fraction of an inch. 'Certainly. I love it here.' And I've no intention whatever of letting *anyone* run me out of town.

He nodded, seemingly satisfied. 'If you will excuse me, *mademoiselle*, I see someone over there I must speak to.'

When he had gone, she launched herself into a series of vivacious, meaningless little conversations. She was joining in the laughter at a joke she had only half understood, when the laugh died on her lips as she saw, across the room, Alain, apparently oblivious to her and everyone else and deep in conversation with—surely she recognised that blonde nape?

The woman half turned her head. Yes, it was Sophie Larbaud. Jassy felt her lips tighten on a peculiar little grimace of pain, but then, just at that moment, Alain looked directly across at her over Sophie's bare shoulder, a cold, hostile stare. She turned away, feeling the tears already standing in her eyes, then, terrified that Martine might be still looking on from some hidden vantage-point, she blotted them away with another long gulp of champagne.

This just wasn't the way she had dreamed this evening would be: a glittering reception in one of the top hotels in France, if not the world—once, the beloved palace of Louis Napoleon's empress, Eugénie, and later the summer residence for half the crowned—and uncrowned—heads of Europe. It should have been one of the most excitiing evenings of her life, and she should have spent it at Alain's side, happily helping him fly the Deville flag.

And now *he* had ruined it. If only he had offered her some explanation, instead of so cavalierly brushing aside her questions and her hurt. She stared broodingly down into her glass, slowly swirling the pale gold liquid. . . She should have heeded her own warnings about never allowing herself to get involved with——

'Mademoiselle Powers, I believe?'

'Yes, that's right.'

Startled, Jassy swung round to meet the young, pleasantly smiling man who was standing just behind her. He held out his hand and as she took it she said apologetically, 'I'm sorry—should I know you?'

'No, we have not met. My name is Troubert— Bernard Troubert.'

A burly man cannoned into both of them, knocking them slightly off balance so that they both spilt a few drops of their drinks. Troubert scowled at the retreating back. 'What an oaf—one of our golfing friends, no doubt.'

They exchanged slightly conspiratorial smiles.

'So you're on the perfume side of this do as well, are you?' Jassy asked.

'That's right. I'm in marketing.'

Light dawned—he must be the new marketing director Alain had told her about.

'So you're down from Paris?'

'Yes.' He grimaced. 'I felt I had to be here tonight. I don't normally go for these occasions, but they're part of the job. To be quite truthful, I was not looking forward to it, but now I have a feeling that I am going to enjoy myself, after all.'

He favoured her with a smile, a white, even-toothed smile, and she stepped back half a pace, colouring slightly under the none too subtle compliment. How hot it was in here, and all at once the room was beginning to gyrate slowly around her.

'Are you all right, Mademoiselle Powers?' Troubert was regarding her closely, his face puckered with concern. 'Let me get you another drink.'

He lifted his hand to beckon a waiter, but Jassy said quickly, 'No, no more for me, thank you.'

As he took a glass for himself, she studied him covertly. She wasn't at all sure that she cared over much for Monsieur Troubert's particular brand of charm, but this was perhaps the automatic stock in trade of the young, upwardly mobile marketing man—and he had to be good at his job, or Alain would never have appointed him. So she had to make an effort.

'And you're the one who's going to help put Deville back on the map.'

'I suppose you could put it like that,' he said guardedly.

'What do you think of the company from what you've seen of it so far?'

'Very impressive.' His tone was still slightly wary, and Jassy warmed to him a little. At least he could not be accused of being indiscreet.

'It's all right,' she reassured him. 'I know all about the new perfume we're bringing out.'

'Ah.' He seemed to relax visibly. 'Well, in that case, we can speak more freely. You really think it's going to be a world-beater?'

'Well, Alain certainly hopes so.' She gave a rather self-conscious laugh. 'And what do you think about the name?'

'The name? It has been finally settled, then?'

'Well, I thought so. We——'

She stopped abruptly. Surely Alain had told him—if not, it could only mean that he had changed his mind about the name, or was at the very least having second thoughts. And if he was having second thoughts about that——

Just then, a little space in the swirling crowd

cleared at the far end of the room and she glimpsed Alain again. He was talking to a group of men now, but when he caught sight of her he stopped in mid-sentence. His eyes went swiftly from her to the man beside her, then back again, his face freezing into a scowl of fury at them both.

Bernard Troubert, his back half turned from him, was enjoying his drink in blissful ignorance of that killing look, but Jassy's heart leapt to her throat for a moment with sheer terror. But then she thought angrily, What the heck—he'd been closeted in a cosy tête-á-tête with Sophie for half the evening, hadn't he, so it was sauce for the gander.

She scowled back at him, then, with a defiant toss of her copper curls, turned back to her companion.

'I imagine you're going to be kept very busy over the next——'

Her voice trembled into silence as, out of the very corner of her eye, she saw Alain disengage himself from the group and, his face pale beneath the suntan, make towards them. He was halfway across the room and Jassy, dry-mouthed, was still trying to make up her mind whether to stand her ground or flee in terror, when a man put a detaining hand on his arm.

For a second she thought he was going to shake it off, but then, at the same moment, an announcement came from the platform that Alain Deville would now present the trophies to the prize-winners. Amid the little ripple of applause, Jassy watched him turn reluctantly and make his way up to the stage.

He ran through the ceremony with smooth

efficiency, and yet she was quite certain that all the time at least half his mind was on the corner of the room where she was standing. As soon as the last cup and cheque had been presented, with the barest nod as acknowledgement of the final round of applause, he leapt lightly down from the platform and headed purposefully in their direction again.

This time, she knew there would be no reprieve, and when she glanced swiftly at Bernard Troubert she saw that he too was watching Alain approach with distinct unease. Even so, as Alain came up to them, he put out his hand.

'Deville. Good to see you again.'

Alain ignored the hand totally.

'What the hell are you doing here, Troubert?'

The blazing anger was vibrating from him and Jassy realised that he could barely keep his hands off them both.

'Alain——' she began.

'Keep out of this!' he snapped, without even glancing at her. 'Well, Troubert?'

'Oh, you know.' The other man made a weak attempt at a careless smile. 'Always interested in how Deville are getting on.'

Alain swore crudely, then, obviously becoming aware of pricked ears all round them, said in a low voice, 'Either you leave of your own accord, or I throw you out—now.'

'If you insist, old man.' He set down his glass and turned to Jassy, who was staring at him in utter bewilderment. '*Au revoir*, Mademoiselle Powers. It has been a most—illuminating evening. I look forward to continuing our acquaintance another time.'

And then, as Alain moved threateningly towards him, he turned swiftly on his heel and was gone.

Any cowardly hope that Alain might have expended all his anger on the unfortunate Troubert was short-lived. He swung round to her, his face a cold mask.

'Right, now for you. We're leaving.'

'Alain dear!' Through the champagne haze which was enveloping her, Jassy heard the sugared tones of Monique, as she put a hand on her nephew's arm. 'There are some people here you simply must meet.'

'Sorry.' He brusquely shook himself free. 'You see them—after all, you never tired of telling Armand how well you could run the company.'

Ignoring her purse-lipped displeasure, he caught Jassy by the wrist and, oblivious to the curious stares all round them, half led, half dragged her from the room, along the corridor to the entrance hall, her feet pattering helplessly over the enormous carpet, with its royal NE cartouches, then out past the astonished commissionaires to the car.

'L-let me go, damn you,' she panted. 'You're hurting me!'

'Good,' he snarled, then, jerking open the door, almost threw her in.

Before she could do more than seize the handle in a futile attempt to escape, he was beside her, had switched on the engine, reversed at top speed and they were roaring down the drive.

At the gates, he swung into the Avenue de l'Impératrice and she thought at first that they were heading for his villa, but he raced past the turning, breaking every traffic regulation in the book, and

finally halted with a vicious jab on the brakes in the
deserted car park on the headland alongside the
lighthouse.

'Now.' He swivelled round on her, his dark bulk
full of menace in the confined space, so that she
edged away from him as far as she could. 'Just how
much did you tell that swine back there?'

'Tell?' Jassy stared at him blankly. 'I didn't tell
him anything.'

'You mean to say, you told him nothing about our
new perfume?'

'Well, I mentioned it, of course. But he knows
about that already.'

Her fingers were clenching and unclenching in her
lap and, unable to bear the naked hostility in his
face, she averted her eyes to gaze out through the
windscreen at the black sea beneath them.

'Look, Alain, I don't know what this is all about,
but I was only talking to him for a couple of minutes,
and I said nothing, I swear it. But what does it
matter, anyway?'

'What does it matter?' he mimicked her cruelly.
'Look at me, damn you!'

Putting his hand under her chin, he brutally
wrenched her head round towards him. A pale beam
from the lighthouse flickered past them, briefly
illuminating their faces and giving his eyes the cold
sheen of steel.

'You're either a naïve little fool or even more
unscrupulous than I first took you for. And we both
know you're not naïve, so——' He let the sentence
hang between them, then went on with even greater
savagery, 'I said that day when we first met that

every woman has her price—remember? So—how much was he offering you?'

Jassy moistened her dry lips with the tip of her tongue. For a moment, back in the salon, she'd thought that his fury had been caused by jealousy and she had been almost glad, but there was no jealousy here—just an icy contempt, which froze her. If only she could think straight, but that fourth glass of champagne was really befuddling her brain. And, in any case, Alain was clearly almost beyond reasoning with, but she had to make one more desperate attempt.

'Alain, I truly have no idea what you're talking about. Just what is it about this Bernard Troubert?' But then a terrible thought broke through the alcohol daze and she asked, almost pleadingly, 'He—he does work for us, doesn't he?'

'He did—once. Until Armand fired him for selling our secrets to the highest bidder—as if you didn't know.' He laughed bitterly. 'That day at the factory, when I warned you about industrial espionage—I think *I* must be the naïve fool.'

Oh God! Troubert, not a Deville employee, but a spy! And just what had she said to him? She trawled frantically through her befuddled brain. That was right—she'd been on the point of telling him——

'But you can't possibly believe this of me—that I would do s-such a thing,' she whispered.

'Can't I? I rather think, *chérie*, that my first estimate of you has proved more than correct, after all. Out of sheer malice—no, pique—at being deprived of your little treat of a trip to New York, you decided to pay me back in the best way possible.'

Her heart was being broken inside her, without anaesthetic, but somehow she must hide from him the pain he was so callously inflicting. She set her head proudly, to meet his eyes without flinching.

'I think you've said enough, Alain. Will you take me home, please?'

'Gladly.' He released his grip on her, thrusting her away as though he could not bear to touch her. 'But let me just say this. If ever I catch you with Troubert again, I'll break every bone in his body and then start on you!'

He started the car, then swung it in a huge arc back on to the road. Jassy pressed herself back in her seat, fighting despairingly to contain the enormous sob which she knew must burst from her at any second. He shouldn't see her cry—he must not.

The road was crowded now with late-night revellers and as Alain, caught up in the snarl of traffic, was forced to brake sharply, she wrenched open her door and leapt out. Barely aware of the angry shouts from the startled drivers around her, she ran across the road, darting among the cars, then, with a little gasp of relief, saw just beside her the long, dark flight of steps which led down to the Miramar beach.

She rammed her clenched fist to her mouth, but then, half blinded by the tears which were streaming freely now, she launched herself headlong down them.

CHAPTER TEN

JASSY had reached almost halfway when, above her own laboured breathing, she heard running footsteps behind her. Alain—it had to be him.

She skidded to a halt. There was no way she could outrun him, even if she took off her high-heeled shoes. Staring wildly around her, she saw just ahead an open gateway. Of course—the garden of that derelict clifftop house.

In her trembling anxiety, she was hardly aware of the jagged fragments of wood from the broken-down gate as she scrambled through it. To one side, there was an overgrown buddleia bush and, stumbling through the unkempt grass, she crouched down in its dense shade, her breath bursting in her lungs.

Just the other side of the wall, those racing footsteps stopped, then Alain called, 'Jassy! Where the hell are you?'

His voice crackled with anger, and seconds later she sensed rather than saw his outline framed in the entrance. She almost melted into the shrub, biting savagely into her mouth to stop the shuddering breath. She felt his eyes scan the steep garden; they raked across the bush, then as she stopped breathing altogether they seemed to pause, before, with a furious exclamation, he turned away and she heard him going slowly back up the steps.

She waited, hunched into herself and hugging her

knees, until the sound had died away and then, straining her ears to their utmost, she caught, far above her, a car door slamming. Only then did she straighten up stiffly and climb back through the gate.

The pale ribbon of beach was deserted and, kicking off her shoes, she walked the length of it, her feet scuffing the fine sand, and almost oblivious of the incoming tide dragging at the hem of her dress. Through the numb misery that was creeping through her, she registered that her left arm was stinging, and when she looked down at it she saw, quite without emotion, a long, jagged scratch, from which blood was trickling.

Only when she could follow the beach no further did she walk up through the town, utterly careless of the curious glances she was attracting, and finally back to the Villa Chantal. She had been half afraid to venture down the shadowed avenue, in case a grey Citroën was lying in wait by the front entrance, but the drive was deserted.

In the hall, though, she came face to face with Céline, in a voluminous dressing-gown.

'Oh, Mademoiselle Jacinth, what is it? Has there been an accident?'

But Jassy, her flayed spirit cringing from any display of sympathy, could only manage a tight-faced shake of the head and, after a tiny moment's hesitation, Céline hurried away upstairs.

Jassy went on into the sitting-room and hunched on the sofa, her chin to her knees, staring at the pattern of moonlight that lay across the carpet in long silver ingots. Her face was set into a taut mask and inside, her stomach was a tight, clenched fist of misery. She desperately wanted the release of tears, but now that she was free to cry it was as though the pain had turned inward on her and lay, too deep for tears.

She leaned back, still watching the moonlight with blank eyes. There was something almost soothing about that shifting, blurring pattern. . .

The ormolu clock was striking seven and one of the maids was already moving around in the kitchen. Every muscle in Jassy's body was stiff and aching, her arm throbbed, but her mind, miraculously, was clear. She had to speak to Alain, explain, reach out to him across this terrible gulf that had opened up between them. Now, before it was too late.

She was already at the phone, dialling his number. Look, Alain, she'd say, I know I was incredibly stupid last night, but that was just the champagne. I swear I'd no idea who he was, and anyway, I told him nothing. And then he'll say——

But it was his housekeeper—Marie, was she called?—who told her that Monsieur had left, just a quarter of an hour before.

'No, *madame*, it was nothing of any importance.'

Jassy replaced the receiver with careful exactness and went slowly upstairs.

'*Mademoiselle, mademoiselle*!' As Jassy swung round, startled, the young assistant caught her by the arm. 'You forgot your change.'

'Oh, how silly of me. Thank you.'

She stuffed the money into her purse and hurried away through the department store. Oh God, would she never shake herself out of this? Every evening, for almost a week now, she had vowed to herself that she would take the next morning by the scruff of its neck, but then, when she woke, pale and heavy-eyed, she would listlessly drag herself through yet another endless day.

And it was the second time this afternoon that she'd made a fool of herself. Earlier, she had been looking at—or rather, looking straight through—a rack of jewellery in a boutique down in the Port Vieux, then, finding herself in the doorway, still clutching a gold filigree chain, she had caught the openly suspicious gaze of the shopkeeper and hurriedly replaced it, before fleeing in scarlet-faced embarrassment.

She had wandered into the perfume department now, frowning as she struggled to remember something very important. Then, as she saw the Deville stand, she thought, Of course, I must tell Alain that he's not to use my name for the new perfume. . . But supposing he won't give in, says it's too late? Well then, perhaps I can copyright it. . . A feeble little giggle rose in her, but then died. Of course, I needn't worry—he surely won't want to call it Jassy now, in any case. . .

Huge banners suspended from the ceiling proclaimed the imminent approach of *la Rentrée*, urging the varied delights of the store's Back to School wear. It was still August, but autumn would soon be here. Autumn in England—crisp days, walks crunching through dry leaves, muffins toasting in front of an open fire for weekend tea. . .

A wholly unexpected wave of homesickness filled

her with such desolation that for a few moments she could only stand on the pavement, heedlessly allowing herself to be buffeted along by the crowds. Finally, she found herself standing outside the Salon de Thé. Of course, an English-type tea-room. Pots of English tea and cream cakes—in the sudden mood of sharp nostalgia that had overwhelmed her, it seemed the perfect self-indulgent combination, the one thing that just might lift her from her trough of despair.

The place was almost empty and Jassy made for a table near the window, but then, realising that she would see the lighthouse—and perhaps *his* villa— from there, she turned away abruptly, almost cannoning into someone just behind her.

'Why, Jassy! How good to see you!'

Dazed, she stared at the other woman, then finally registered that it was Martine.

'You are having tea? How nice. We'll have it together—and you must be my guest. No,' as Jassy tried to protest feebly, 'I insist.'

So, too weary to argue, and in any case, in this mood of utter desolation, grateful for any human company—Martine's, even, seemed preferable to her own—Jassy submitted, allowing herself to be led to the counter to choose her gâteau, and then to be escorted to a table for two.

While they waited for the tea to be brought, Jassy was more than content to let Martine hijack the conversation. She had been shopping and regaled her with a lively account of an amusing incident involving a miniature poodle in the changing-rooms at Hermès' boutique.

Away from her mother, she was emerging as a pleasant companion, and Jassy began to wonder whether she had misjudged her. When the tea arrived, Martine poured for them both, then, dropping a slice of lemon into her own cup, she stirred it gently around.

'I'm so glad we've met like this, Jassy—you don't mind if I call you that?'

Through the numbing misery that still enveloped her, Jassy roused herself to shake her head. 'No, of course not, Martine.'

'I was hoping to have a chat with you at the reception the other night, but when I looked for you, you'd gone.'

That pierced the blank wall of unhappiness, and Jassy's head jerked up sharply, but Martine's face was smoothly expressionless above her tea cup, so she only said, 'Oh, I'm sorry, but I left early—I had a headache.'

'Yes,' Martine nodded sympathetically, 'it was unbearably hot, wasn't it? But anyway, I know we got off to such an unfortunate start, but as two of the younger generation of the Deville board, we really ought to become friends.'

'But I thought you were hoping to—give up your interest in the company?' This seemed to Jassy the most tactful way of putting it.

'That's true. We were, but now, with Alain in charge, we are all confident that he can pull the firm round. My cousin is such a livewire, isn't he?'

Jassy, unable to trust her voice, could only nod in agreement.

'But having established such a close working relationship with him, you'd know that, of course.'

'Yes, well, we. . .' Jassy's voice mumbled to a
halt.

'And we have high hopes of this latest New York
visit. It's a sales promotion, presumably?'

So Alain hadn't really taken *them* into his confidence, after all. Jassy's spirits rose a fraction.

'They make such a brilliant team, don't they?'

'They?' The word was out before Jassy could even
wish she had held her tongue.

'He and Sophie Larbaud, of course.'

Half the contents of Jassy's teacup lurched out
into her saucer. 'Sophie?'

'But of course.' Martine peered closely into her
face, then went on solicitously, 'Oh dear, didn't you
know? I assumed that he would have told you that
Sophie was going with him.' She spread her hands
apologetically. 'I mean, she always does accompany
him on these trips.' She smiled indulgently. 'They
say that business and pleasure never mix, but those
two seem to manage it very well, don't they?'

So it was true. All her black suspicions, which she
had tried so hard to dismiss. . .

'They've been lovers for years, of course,'
Martine's voice was going smoothly on. 'Very dis-
creet. But with Sophie based in Paris——'

Jassy stood up. From somewhere deep inside
herself, she found the strength to face the other
woman.

'Thank you for the tea, Martine—we must do it
again some time. But I have an appointment in ten
minutes, so I really have to go.'

And forcing her stiff features into a semblance of a smile, she left.

Somehow, she reached the sea front and wandered along, scarcely aware of the holiday crowds around her, until she reached the steps that led to the old fishing port.

Once down below, she leaned her elbows on the wall, watching without seeing a small boat unloading its catch of glistening sardines. Gradually, the nausea which had gripped her as she had stared helplessly into Martine's cold eyes abated, and at the same time that paralysis that had so numbed her mind for days past retreated, leaving her brain clear and ice-cold.

Of course, Martine had followed her into the tea-room. Just as a jackal will stake out the weakest member of a herd, so she, by some predatory instinct, had sensed Jassy's vulnerability and moved in for the kill. How much she knew about her relationship with Alain—or his promise of the New York trip—Jassy could not guess, but she must, at the very least, have realised her growing attraction for him and had set out, quite ruthlessly, to wound her, or even better, to drive her away.

But why should she care? After all, she had already suspected that Sophie meant far more to Alain than merely a highly efficient sales director, and in any case—once again—why should she care? OK, she'd launched herself heedlessly into a passionate affair, but she'd had that one wonderful, stolen weekend with him, so—remember the rules of the game, she told herself sternly. It's over now and it's time to shed those few tears and walk away, still in one piece.

But I'm not in one piece, she thought, as weak tears filled her eyes. He's broken my heart and I shall never put it together again. Oh, for heaven's sake—her other, tougher self was jeering at her—don't be so pathetic! Of course you will. He's just a man, isn't he—and a rat, into the bargain?

But I love him, she whimpered, and put her head down on her arms. No, you don't, her other self protested, horrified. Jacinth Powers, you cannot possibly love such an arrogant, selfish, *cruel* swine as that.

I do, she thought sadly, then sniffed as a large tear slid down her cheek. I've loved him since—oh, long before that weekend, from way back. She frowned to herself—yes, since that day of the surfing lesson, only she had refused to recognise the feeling for what it was, refused to admit that when she was with him the sun shone, and when he was absent, she was only half alive.

But you've been in love before—or thought you were—and got over it, haven't you? No, it was nothing like this—the pain, the anguish, the desolation.

How blind, how stupid she'd been! To get involved with a man like Alain Deville was crazy enough, but to do it, loving him yet knowing that he would never love her, had been sheer madness. And yet, for just that one weekend, he too seemed to have been infected with the same madness. Three days back in Paris, though, had been enough to bring him to his senses. . .

A group of children armed with shrimping nets ran past, so close that one brushed against her, and she roused herself. Well? That other little voice, now cold with self-contempt, was whispering to her again. Now that you know the truth, what do you intend doing about it?

Leave Biarritz. The answer leapt to her mind. But how can I bear never to see him again? Her face screwed up against the piercing stab that shot through her vitals, but then, as the pain ebbed just a little, she forced herself upright and began walking rapidly back towards town.

Even when she was actually on the doorstep of Marcel Ridoux's office, she still had no clear thought of why she had come here and what she was going to do. Only when, probably alarmed by her white, set face, his clerk summoned the lawyer from discussions with another client, did she know what she must say.

'Monsieur Ridoux.' Automatically, she held out her hand to him, speaking through rigid lips which could scarcely formulate the words. 'I'm very sorry to disturb you——' for a moment, the old, polite Jassy took control '—but I have to see you. I am returning to England as soon as possible——' she paused, frowning slightly as momentarily she lost the thread of what she was saying and could only repeat '—as soon as possible.'

'But, Mademoiselle Powers——'

'I am relinquishing my interest in Deville. I shall keep the proceeds of the sale of the Villa Chantal— though only because Armand would wish it,' she added quickly, with a little spurt of pride. 'I shall leave it in your hands, of course, to make sure that Céline and the staff do not suffer in the least. And I am handing over my shareholding to——' she could not quite get the name out '—to Alain Deville.'

'Handing over?' Monsieur Ridoux sounded as if he too was having difficulty formulating his words.

'Yes.' So that there should be absolutely no misunderstanding by anyone, she added firmly, 'Giving them to him—free.'

The remnants of the lawyer's smooth professional façade cracked wide open, but then, as shock horror chased itself across his face, he made a desperate effort.

'But—but, *mademoiselle*, you cannot possibly do this! I must insist—I cannot permit you——'

If she stayed here a moment longer her own self-control would splinter in front of him.

'I'm sorry, Monsieur Ridoux. I know it will make things very difficult for you, but my mind is made up. What's today?' She pressed two fingers to her throbbing temple. 'Thursday. There's a direct flight to London on Saturday afternoon and I intend to be on it.'

'But, *mademoiselle*,' he seemed to be almost weeping with anguish, 'you cannot be so precipitate! At least wait until Monsieur Alain returns, so that he——'

'*No!*' Wait for the very man who was driving her away? Jassy put a hand on his arm. 'Please, it's better this way, believe me. If there are any—any papers to be signed, please send them round to me before Saturday.'

Then as her voice broke, she turned and fled.

Better this way, better this way. Her own words were echoing in her brain as she made her way back to the villa. Would Monsieur Ridoux, even now, be making a frantic call to New York? What would Alain do, what would he think? He'd be highly delighted, no doubt—after all, she was handing him on a plate what he had wanted so badly all along. And maybe even that joyous weekend had only been part of his campaign, as coldly and skilfully planned as any other.

As she let herself in, she heard Céline and one of the maids talking in the kitchen. She would have to see them soon, but not yet—she couldn't face anyone now.

In her bedroom, she stood by the window for a long time, resting her head on her hand and looking out across the garden. But at last she roused herself and, opening the wardrobe, began methodically lifting out her clothes. It was far too early to pack, of course, but she had to fill her mind with something. . .

There were piles of clothes arranged neatly on the bed: underwear, beachwear, sweaters, dresses. There was just one thing left in the wardrobe—the peacock-blue dress she had worn that night of the reception. She took it down, then, as she folded it, dimly, through her stupor, she heard loud exclamations below, running footsteps, a furious voice.

'Jassy! Where the hell are you?'

She clutched at the dress. Her mind was giving way—she was hallucinating, cowering once more on those dark steps. But then, as the footsteps came nearer, she flung the dress down and leapt towards the half-open door.

Putting her hand flat against it, she tried to bang it to, but then, on the other side, someone gave it a savage jerk that sent it crashing back and her reeling away. As she slumped against the wall, one hand to her throat, her eyes wide with terror, Alain erupted into the room.

CHAPTER ELEVEN

ALAIN slammed the door shut behind him, flung on to the bed a manila folder he was carrying, and advanced on Jassy. There was a flush of temper on his cheekbones and his eyes sparkled with fury.

'What the hell are you up to, you little idiot?' Then, as Jassy stared at him, stunned into silence, 'I've a good mind to get a hold of you and——'

His arms came out towards her, but then, as she shrank back almost into the wallpaper, he winced and put a hand up to his neck.

'What's the matter? You've hurt yourself.' She straightened up and took a tentative step towards him.

'Nothing whatever is the matter,' he snarled, 'except you, of course. Nothing has *ever* been the matter with me, except you, since the day I met you.'

'Well, thank you,' Jassy retorted, with a flash of her old spirit.

'I cut short my trip to New York—leaving all sorts of things half finished,' he was still nursing his neck, 'call off on Ridoux, to find that you are all set to sneak off like some thief in the night, without——'

Anger was rapidly displacing her stupefaction. After all he'd said—all he'd done, how dared he come storming in here, venting his foul temper on her?

'I am *not* sneaking off, but I am going back to England. I'm catching the——'

'And what's all this nonsense about your shares?'

'It is not nonsense,' she said stiffly. 'I meant what I said to him, so there's no need for you to worry about the shares any more.'

'Oh, — the shares!' Jassy was glad that she did not understand the expletive. 'And as for your leaving, I am telling you that you are not going *anywhere*, and that is final—finish—end of conversation.'

Jassy's fractured nerves splintered finally into fury.

'And I'm telling you, I damn well am going, and— and you can stuff your stupid shares! *No*——' as he made a determined lunge at her '—don't you dare lay a finger on me!' But then, 'Oh, Alain, what's wrong?' as, very pale suddenly, he dropped on to the bed, cradling his neck in his hand.

She went across and knelt beside him. His eyes were half closed, there was a film of sweat on his upper lip and, surely—she gently moved aside his hair—yes, there was a long, purpling bruise across his temple.

'H-have you been in an accident?' Her voice was not quite steady.

'Not exactly!' His eyes were still half closed. 'There was a fire in one of the plane's engines—it had to make an emergency landing, and we all came down the chute. I brought down a couple of kids with me, as their mother was scared to death.'

'And you broke their fall, I suppose?' Jassy said huskily. 'Didn't a doctor check you?'

Alain waved an irritable hand. 'Didn't want to wait.'

She stared at him and, at the thought of what might so easily have happened, the sickness welled inside her. She ached to pull him into the shelter of her arms, but, not daring to allow herself even to think of that, took refuge instead in brisk professionalism.

'Come on.' She stood up. 'Let's have a look at you.'

'What?'

'Well,' she managed a shaky smile, 'I am a fully trained physiotherapist, remember.'

And before he could protest, she had slipped her hand under his elbow, had raised him to his feet and was steering him through the door.

'Where are we going?'

'To the treatment-room I used for Armand. It's still set up. No—*be quiet*,' as he started to argue, 'and no, you certainly are not having a drink—you may need an anaesthetic later. I'll at least be able to see what the damage is, and whether you need to go to hospital.'

She helped him off with his jacket, then as he began to struggle with his tie she gently put his hands aside and unknotted it, then unbuttoned his shirt and got him out of it, all the time carefully avoiding any eye contact.

You're doing fine, she told herself, just fine. Go on treating him like any patient in great pain and you'll get over him all the faster. But then, as she straightened up from adjusting the bed, she saw that he had kicked off his shoes and was stripping down to navy boxer shorts. As she stared at that tanned, well-muscled back, terrible feelings warred inside her, but then—— *No*. Remember that it's only a body, *any* body, in need of your healing skills.

'Oh, very professional,' he said snappishly, his eyes taking in the white coat she was just fastening.

But she only said, coolly impersonal, 'Now, let me help you up. I want you lying on your front, please.'

And—almost—entirely closing her mind to the touch of her fingers on that smooth, silky body, which so recently she had held in passionate embrace, she pulled down the powerful overhead light and began her careful examination. . .

'Well,' she said, in her most clinical manner, as she broke a silence that had gone on for at least ten minutes, 'you've been very lucky. There's no spinal damage, and you haven't even a dislocation. It's just an extremely severe muscular spasm. Of course,' she added, with a hint of asperity aimed at the back of his silent head, 'you don't have to take my word for it. I'm not letting you drive again, but I'll be happy to take you to hospital—that is, if you trust me with that beautiful Citroën of yours.'

'No, thanks, Miss Bossyboots.' His voice was muffled by the pillow. 'So, what can *you* do for me?'

'Well, I can give you heat treatment and some massage. Very gentle, of course—nothing probing today.'

'And what about tomorrow?'

Tomorrow? Jassy thought of saying that she would be far too busy packing, but instead, 'I'll give you another deeper massage, then, if you like, to start unknotting those muscles.' She put a hand very gently on his tight shoulder.

'And how long shall I look like Quasimodo for?'

'Oh, no more than a few days, I should think. You must rest it, of course——'

'In that case, you'll have to amuse me. I get very bored doing nothing.'

How could he? She stared disbelievingly down at his averted face. He'd left Sophie, perhaps only hours before, and now—— She bit her lip against the angry pain, then forced herself to become coolly professional once more.

'But I can give you a little gentle massage— *effleurage*—now, to ease it slightly.'

She poured some massage oil into her palm, then dribbled it across his shoulder.

'Ouch, that's cold!' Alain winced.

Good, she thought, and set to work, gently coaxing a little of the tension out of those taut muscles. . .

'Ah,' he gave a little sigh of relief, 'that's better.' Then, his voice still muffled against the pillow, 'Well, don't you want to know how we got on?'

Jassy's busy fingers stilled for an instant. 'We?'

'Mmm. Sophie and I in New York. Ow, that hurt!' He tried to scowl round at her.

'Oh, I'm *so* sorry.'

But she wasn't, not at all. He was obviously so filled with male conceit that he actually thought he could flagrantly flaunt Sophie's name in front of her and at the same time take up again with her the process of keeping himself temporarily 'amused'.

'Yes,' he went on, seemingly oblivious of her

pent-up emotions, 'Sophie thinks she will really enjoy working over there.'

Jassy's fingers stilled again. 'She—she's going to work in New York?'

'That's right.' His voice was entirely devoid of expression. 'She's taking over as our North American sales director.'

'She's——?'

'And the preliminary work on the Jassy perfume is going well. The agency agrees with me——'

Her mind was tottering, but there was something she urgently had to tell him. 'Oh, but, Alain, I've decided that I don't want——'

'—that it will be a fabulous idea for you to model it in the ads.'

'Model it!' Jassy gave up all pretence of massaging him and stood, staring open-mouthed at his face, still half buried in the pillow. 'But—but that's impossible! I-I've never modelled anything in my life. And besides,' she was clutching at a straw, 'they don't even know what I look like——'

'Oh, I've told them. And anyway, you remember those Polaroid pictures I took of you?'

She could only nod. He had taken them in his garden on that Monday afternoon, before taking her back home after that one magical weekend.

'Well, I showed them to the agency guys—told them that they didn't do you justice, of course, and they——'

'But I——' Jassy's mind was reeling.

'—also agree whole-heartedly with me that all we need to make it a world-beater is for it to be modelled, not by Jassy Powers, but by Jassy Deville.'

As she braced her hands flat on the table to stop her legs crumbling away beneath her, he went on, 'And let me tell you that only the dazzling prospect of those chart-topping sales figures will persuade me to marry an evil-tempered, vicious-tongued little termagant like you.' He reached round for one of her hands and, pulling it to him, held it to his lips. 'Well, say something, my adorable Jassy,' he murmured against her palm.

'But—but Sophie,' she began helplessly.

He rolled over very gingerly on to his back and looked up at her, his eyes narrowing. 'What about Sophie?'

'Well, you took her with you to New York, instead of me. And—and I know all about your affair.'

Alain jerked upright, then slumped back with a groan of pain. 'Sit down, for God's sake. You're giving me another crick in the neck!'

Her brain was only half functioning, but she reluctantly pulled up a chair beside him.

'Now, has that bloody aunt of mine been getting at you?'

'Well——' at the blaze of fury in his eyes, she faltered '—actually it was Martine. She told me that you'd taken Sophie with you and that——' she stopped to steady her voice '—that you've been having an affair with her for years. Every time you go up to Paris or on overseas trips, she. . .'

As her voice tailed away, he took her hand again and held it, gently rubbing his thumb across the back. 'Jassy, you must believe me. I swear to you that there has never been anything physical between Sophie and me. I've known, liked and respected her for a long time, but that something—that spark which, whether I liked it or not, and I certainly didn't at first,' he gave her a wry smile, 'has been between us two from the beginning, was always missing—for my part, at least——'

He broke off, frowning as though at some painful memory. 'When I went back to Paris last week, I told her I was going to marry you. The New York job was vacant, and I'd already thought about offering it to her, but then—well, she asked if she could have it. And that's why she went with me.'

'But—but why didn't you tell me?'

Alain grimaced. 'I thought at first of taking you with me as well, but that would have looked as if I was parading you in front of her, and I didn't want to hurt her any more. Although, of course, I just ended up hurting you instead.'

Jassy squeezed his hand gently. 'I would have understood, really I would, Alain.'

'I know. I just completely mishandled the whole thing. Early on at the reception, I'd made up my mind to tell you, but then, when I saw you with Troubert—well, I just flipped my lid. Above all, I think, I was furious with myself for falling in love with you, when it looked as if you really were that unscrupulous little gold-digger. Jassy,' his voice was very sombre, 'please forgive me. I, more than anyone, should know that you are utterly incapable of anything mean or underhand.'

Pure joy was flooding through her, sweeping away

all the pain and grief, but all she could say was, 'Yes, Alain, of course I do.'

Gently, he kissed her hand again. 'I came back early because of the way I'd left you—and because,' he gave her a mock-rueful smile, 'I cannot keep away from you. But I also wanted to tell you——'

'Yes?' she prompted softly.

'Well, among other things, that I love you, adore you, am crazy about you,' and the look he gave her made her throat tighten as though a hand had gripped it, 'but I wanted you to know that I've decided to put my electronics business in Paris up for sale so that I can buy out Monique and the others. You and I between us can always outvote them——'

'Oh, you're so sure now that I'll always be on your side, are you?' Jassy demanded teasingly.

He laughed. 'Well, of course, it will be your duty, as a subservient little wife, to do my every bidding, now that I'm such a very sick man, but,' as she looked threateningly at him, 'I'm tired of the constant running battle with them. Besides which, after Martine's latest little exploit, I'm not at all sure that I can be trusted to be in the same room with her.'

'But you haven't asked me yet.'

'Asked you what?'

'To marry you, of course.'

'Oh, haven't I? I thought I had. Although, my sweet, maybe I am rather wary of a direct proposal.' Alain rolled his eyes. 'The last time, I seem to remember, you went straight for my jugular—and I've still got the scars to prove it.' He rubbed his jaw reminiscently. 'But maybe I'll take a chance, just this once. Mademoiselle Powers, will you marry me?'

'Oh yes, Monsieur Deville, if you insist.' Then, as he drew her to him, she whispered tremulously, 'Oh, Alain, I've missed you so much!'

The telephone ringing made them leap apart, and Jassy picked up the extension.

'Yes, Monsieur Ridoux, he's still here.'

She held out the receiver to Alain. He eased himself off the bed, listened for a moment, then, 'No, I haven't had a chance to look through it yet. . . In any case, I'll be calling on you again shortly, to draw up a marriage settlement. . .' He laughed. 'Yes, that's right, Jassy and I. . . What?' There was a long silence as Alain listened intently, firstly disbelief, then astonishment, and finally wry amusement chasing themselves across his face. 'Well, the crafty old devil—I suppose I should have guessed, though. . . Right, I'll see you tomorrow, Marcel. *Au revoir.*'

He put the receiver down and turned to Jassy, a rather odd little smile on his lips. 'Well, when I was proposing to you just now, I didn't realise that I'd had my wife chosen for me.'

When she looked blankly at him, he went on, 'Ridoux says that Armand confided in him that he had decided it was high time I settled down, and, having found the perfect wife for me, he laid his plans accordingly. Hence the will, which did exactly what it was intended to do—throw us together.'

'You mean, the villa, the shares, it was all——' Jassy broke off, shaking her head.

'That's right. And he also told Ridoux that if he'd

been forty years younger, he wouldn't have allowed me within a mile of you.'

'And do you mind—having your wife chosen for you, I mean?' She gave him a demure look.

He spread his hands expressively. 'How could I? Armand always did have impeccable taste in women.'

Jassy smiled sadly. 'Yes, although I don't think he'd known real happiness for a very long time.'

They were silent for a few moments, thinking of the old man and that tragic accident which had robbed him of Chantal, his only real love, then Alain gently brushed her lips with his fingers.

'Don't look like that, my sweet. He wanted us to be happy,' she nodded silently, 'and we shall be, my darling Jassy. Oh, and that reminds me—don't you want to know what my wedding present is to be?' When she looked at him enquiringly, 'Go and fetch that folder I brought with me.'

When she obeyed, he took it. 'This is what Ridoux was ringing about. A new, exclusive resort is being built in Les Landes, north of here, and in the central shopping complex there is to be a small therapy clinic——' he thrust the folder at her '—owned by Jassy Deville.'

As she stared down at it, he went on, 'Well, don't I get a reward?'

'The state you're in?' She gave him a rather blurred smile. 'Certainly not! But thank you, Alain. It's a wonderful present.'

'Of course, you'll have to get a manager—I can't do without you all the time. And besides——' He broke off.

'Besides what?' she asked softly.

'Very soon, I shall want another gorgeous little coppernob—though I hope with a slightly less precarious temper than her mother.'

Jassy, feeling the blush turn her cheeks poppy-red, sought refuge in briskness again, 'Come on. It's high time you were dressed.'

As she bent to pick up his clothes, a white package fell from the jacket pocket.

'Oh, I'd forgotten that. Open it,' he commanded.

The bottle was slim, tinted a misty gold, the white and gold label proclaiming 'Jassy'.

'It's a prototype, but I think we'll use it. I've got some others to show you, though. After all, the final decision must be yours—just on this one occasion, of course.'

Taking the bottle from her, he unscrewed the gold top. 'Now—you remember what Coco Chanel said?'

'Y-yes,' she replied warily, then, as he drew her into his arms and at the same time began, one-handed, to undo her overall, 'No, Alain! You'll hurt your neck.'

'*Yes*, Jassy.' He silenced her with a kiss, then whispered huskily against her lips, 'Listen to me, *ma chère*. First of all, I am going to perfume you all over your beautiful body, and after that—well——'

Delicious quivers were running all through her and, drawing his head down to hers, she kissed him, a long, lingering kiss, which gradually ignited into passion between them. . .

IT'S NEVER TOO LATE FOR SWEET REVENGE . . .

Adrianne's glittering lifestyle was the perfect foil for her extraordinary talents. A modern princess, flitting from one exclusive gathering to another, no one knew her as The Shadow, the most notorious jewel thief of the decade. With a secret ambition to carry out the ultimate heist, Adriane had a spectacular plan — one that would even an old and bitter score. But she would need all her stealth and cunning to pull it off — Philip Chamberlain, Interpol's toughest cop and once a renowned thief himself was catching up with her. His only mistake was to fall under Adrianne's seductive spell.

Published: October 12th　　　　　**Price: £3.50**

W●RLDWIDE

Zodiac Wordsearch
Competition

How would you like a years supply of Mills & Boon Romances ABSOLUTELY FREE?

Well, you can win them! All you have to do is complete the word puzzle below and send it into us by Dec 31st 1990. The first five correct entries picked out of the bag after this date will each win a years supply of Mills & Boon Romances (Six books every month - worth over £100!) What could be easier?

S	E	C	S	I	P	R	I	A	M	F
I	U	L	C	A	N	C	E	R	L	I
S	A	I	N	I	M	E	G	N	S	R
C	A	P	R	I	C	O	R	N	U	E
S	E	I	R	A	N	G	I	S	I	O
Z	O	D	W	A	T	E	R	B	R	I
O	G	A	H	M	A	T	O	O	A	P
D	R	R	T	O	U	N	I	R	U	R
I	I	B	R	O	R	O	M	G	Q	O
A	V	I	A	N	U	A	N	C	A	C
C	E	L	E	O	S	T	A	R	S	S

Pisces	Aries	Leo	Earth	**Please turn over for entry details**
Cancer	Gemini	Virgo	Star	
Scorpio	Taurus	Fire	Sign	
Aquarius	Libra	Water	Moon	
Capricorn	Sagittarius	Zodiac	Air	

How to enter

All the words listed overleaf, below the word puzzle, are hidden in the grid. You can can find them by reading the letters forwards, backwards, up and down, or diagonally. When you find a word, circle it, or put a line through it. After you have found all the words, the left-over letters will spell a secret message that you can read from left to right, from the top of the puzzle through to the bottom.

Don't forget to fill in your name and address in the space provided and pop this page in an envelope (you don't need a stamp) and post it today. Competition closes Dec 31st 1990.

Only one entry per household (more than one will render the entry invalid).

Mills & Boon Competition
Freepost
P.O. Box 236
Croydon
Surrey CR9 9EL

Hidden message _____

_____

Are you a Reader Service subscriber.   Yes ☐   No ☐

Name_____

Address_____

_____

_____

_____ Postcode_____

You may be mailed with other offers as a result of entering this competition.
If you would prefer not to be mailed please tick the box. No ☐   COMP9